WULFGARD™

THE
DEMON'S
FANG

Maegan A. Stebbins

Set in the world of Wulfgard, created by
JUSTIN R.R. STEBBINS
& MAEGAN A. STEBBINS

Cover art and illustrations by Justin R. R. Stebbins

Visit Wulfgard and the author online at:
www.wulfgard.net
www.maverickwerewolf.com

CONTENTS

Horngelgasta
(Geatlings)

Ghost Hill
(Chunni)

Wulfsted
(Wulfings)

Dvergar Gate

Bjornburg
(Bjornings)

The Dwaerrowdowns
(Hill Dwarves)

Baldur's Fjord
(Freylings)

NORTHRIM

Endebraut
Hall

Dark Cliffs

Mimirholt
The Immortal Wood
(Ljosalfar)

Fort Munin
(L. XIX April)

Arrowfall
(Hartwin, Ea)

Kern
(The Forsaken)

Frost Raven Lands

Rimegard
(Skiera, K)

Gryphon Roost
(Kallistos, Ea)

Fort Coldstone
(L. XVI Lupi)

Eloh
(Marks, Ea)

The Forest
of Shadows
(Shadowvale)

Rognosst
Swamp

THE NORTHWESTERN KINGDOM
(PLAINS OF ILLIKON)

Illikon

Artorius
(Rikard, Ea)

(Illikoni, K)

Dragon's Lair
(Drake)

Stonebridge
(Nosenthal, Ea)

Pirgos
(Harroway, C)

Pikeston
(Vulpowicz, C)

THE BLACK LANDS

Kyjovin
(Olgovic, K)

Deltalund
(Van Ryn, K)

THE LOWLANDS

Castle
Greywatch
(Venatori)

Caliha
(Flavius, D)

Blackwall
(Balescu, D)

Blackrock
Foothills

Karak du Vide
(Inquisition)

Edrimark
(Ambrose, D)

Appledale
(Afalon, C)

The Scar

Vyzigord
(Draculea, D)

Pluton Hold
(Plutarch, D)

THE WHITE LANDS

The Iron Pikes
(Iron Gauntlet)

Coronaria
(Doraius, E)

LEGEND:

(EMBLEM)
City Name
(Ruling House)

E = Emperor's Seat
K = Kingdom
D = Dukedom
Ea = Earldom
C = County

Whitehorn
(Caelus, K)

N

Piera
(Skye, D)

Krisa
(Pythia, D)

Goldcrossing

AMPIRE

Templaria
(democracy, K)

Starward
Citadel
(Templars)

OLD ACHAEA
(IMPERIAL HEARTLAND)

Maul Rock
(Centaurs)

Amazonia

Tor Vala

Fort Slaughter
(L. XI Serpentis)

Arcadia
(Lycaos)

Helos
(Lysander, D)

The Southwestern Wilds

Knossos
(Minotaurs)

Cro-Cabra
(Satyrs)

Fort Greenwall
(L. VIII Equestris)

Emerita
(Andallo, K)

Sevenxia
(republic, D)

Justantion
(Ysauria, K)

PART I – Cloak and Dagger

Lightning. Distant flashes periodically lit the tall manor, casting the faces of the many dragons there in an eerie and sudden glow. Thankfully, however, these dragons were made of stone.

The port city called Illikon, crown jewel of the Northwest and seat of power in the wild and untamed outer region of the Achaean Empire, slept peacefully despite the storm at sea. Darkness lay within nearly every building that wasn't an inn or tavern; only the deepest night-life still bustled. Coupled with the stillness of candlelit streets and the gentle waves heard in its seaside districts, the city was nothing short of beautiful.

To the west, the great Castle Illikon overlooked the sprawling docks that held ships from lands local and distant. The keep, with turrets reaching for the heavens and surrounding crenelated walls, appeared starkly modern against the many older-style structures throughout the city below, such as temples to the gods held aloft by tall pillars and alive with pedimental sculptures.

In such an atmosphere, the whole world felt calm and quiet. How could turmoil exist when here rested such a peaceful city?

Peaceful, at least, save for the assassins set on taking a man's life.

Two men crept through the night, scaling the outer, black-iron-bar walls of the noble home. But as they made their way up, before they ascended over and down onto the green manor grounds, the sense of being watched crept up their necks. In the streets nearby, a silhouetted shape stopped. A citizen of Illikon – and he saw them.

He froze. So did the assassins. For half a moment, they looked at each other.

The citizen turned and ran. The taller assassin's hands clenched tighter at the fence they climbed, but the shorter wheeled and leapt from the wall with incredible speed, meeting the cobblestone street in a graceful roll. The tall assassin followed.

"We cannot let him live," said the short one as the tall assassin landed alongside him.

"We can't just *kill* him – we can't leave a trail of bodies," the tall one shot back, but the other assassin gave chase, taking off after their witness. "Niall— get *back* here; we're blown!"

The shorter man, Niall, disappeared around a streetcorner. The tall assassin rose to his full height, eyes scanning buildings along the way. His partner chased the fleeing civilian on foot, but he had other plans.

The tall assassin, Kye Vakurseth – a name he rarely shared due to its obvious unnatural sound – got a running start and leapt up onto the side of a nearby building. He scaled it with ease, finding handholds or else making them with a great gauntlet on his left hand and arm: segmented steel engraved in strange and intricate designs, covered in spikes, and ending with long, metal claws in place of his fingertips.

He pulled himself up onto the roof and set off at a graceful run. With incredible speed, he cleared the gap to the next rooftop. Never once did he slow, gaze focused on the streets...

The civilian still ran. In the distance, a tower loomed. Probably a post of the city watchmen. Kye couldn't let him reach it.

Hot on the man's heels came Niall, rapidly gaining on his target, his long black cloak billowing behind him like a banner of untrustworthiness. Kye, however, overtook them both. He pivoted, jumping from the high rooftop, diving like a falcon – and taking down the unsuspecting civilian.

Kye tackled him, using him to soften his landing, and easily pinned him despite his shouting and flailing.

Kye started, "Be quiet if you know what's good for y—"

Niall didn't pause. He charged straight over, dagger in hand that Kye didn't even notice him drawing, and in a flash, the blade sliced the man's throat. Hot blood sprayed Kye in the face. He reared back, shielding himself from any more of it, and swore an oath in a language unknown to the ears of Men.

The man sputtered and choked, clutching his neck, fingers scrabbling uselessly. Niall watched him suffocate and said, "I told you we cannot let him live. Help me dispose of him once he is a corpse."

Ineffectively wiping his face with his right hand, on which he wore only a fingerless black glove rather than a huge clawed gauntlet, Kye blinked past the blood and glowered at his partner. Niall grabbed the dead civilian under the arms and rapidly hauled the corpse toward an alley. Though his build looked narrow, Niall was remarkably strong.

Kye threw a glance back at the Draconius Manor, the house where their target lived, which they yet again had failed to infiltrate. Walled and intricately decorated, it rose high even over the other rich structures. Gargoyles and grotesques of dragons lined its sides and roof, and a pair of dragon statues flanked the gates of the tall fence surrounding the manor grounds. Candles burned in several windows despite the late hour – with more wicks lit as Kye watched. Someone must've heard or seen something and woken the household. Why did the House of Drake have so many servants, and why were some always awake? Why was their *target* always awake?

They'd languished here for several days, unable to kill the man they sought, and that was far too long.

Kye followed Niall into the darkness of the alley, scanning the area again for any potential witnesses. Thankfully, he saw none, though he did spy some watchmen coming down the way. He squeezed his broad shoulders into the very cramped path Niall had chosen.

"Where are you even planning to hide that?" Kye asked incredulously, keeping his voice low. The stink of blood and death filled his nostrils – it wouldn't be easy to disguise. And he needed to wash his face...

"Perhaps I'll feed it to you," Niall remarked.

Kye fixed him in a flat stare. "Gross."

"Your kind eat flesh, I'm sure."

"I already told you, don't talk about 'my kind.'"

Niall ignored him. "I'll throw the body in the ocean. No one will be the wiser."

"It'll wash up or get caught in a sailor's net..."

"Let *me* handle it. I'm still not impressed with where you hid *your* 'accidental' kill in this forsaken city." He cast Kye a look of daggers over his shoulder. "And wash your face. It's covered in blood."

Kye frowned but did as he was told, muttering as he went, "Yeah, and whose fault is that?"

He departed the alley out the opposite side, letting Niall handle his own dirty-work. He wiped his face as best he could with the cloth he used to clean blood from his blades, making a mental note to wash properly when he got the chance. Moments later, Niall reappeared, skulking alongside him with his dark eyes darting at every shadow.

They made quite a pair. Niall was below average height for an Achaean, a man of the Empire, whereas Kye didn't know his own heritage but stood as tall as the enormous men of Northrim. And while Kye wore a suit of form-fitting and sleeveless black leather that showed his lean and muscular physique, Niall's dark, unremarkable clothing and jerkin left only his face uncovered, his form sinewy and his neck eternally crunched near his shoulders.

Kye led the way back toward the Draconius Manor. He wasn't done studying for tonight. His partner followed him without protest, staying in Kye's sizable shadow. Niall pulled his hood over his head, covering or otherwise shadowing his greasy black hair and patchy yet equally as greasy beard. His features were unpleasant, like the random shapes of a root vegetable but without the comfort of knowing a vegetable was a thing growing beneath the earth, not meant to be gazed upon, rather than a person.

In nearly every way, Kye was Niall's opposite. Clean-shaven, Kye had a handsome and chiseled face, with a strong jaw and a heavy brow to match. Black hair just over shoulder-length was mostly pulled back into a low, loose ponytail over his neck, with only a few strands hanging freely on either side of his face. His white skin carried a subtle nutty hue.

The peculiar duo walked past the manor of the House of Drake again, playing it casual, glancing from afar. Why was it, Kye wondered again, that their target never seemed to rest?

He'd since learned what room belonged to the man he and Niall had been tasked to kill, and it never went without a lit candle, movement, or both. When Kye had first accepted this job – having been hired by a particularly memorable employer who'd worn a mask, all his visible skin slashed by claw-mark scars from great beasts – Kye had foolishly, even arrogantly, expected that killing one knight would prove easy. He'd succeeded in many missions before, some for employers nearly as off-putting.

Yet always his target either remained in the middle of a city that knew him well, surrounded day and night by seasoned soldiers, trained warriors, and veteran knights, or else he traveled far afield on the Plains of Illikon, to distant castles and villages out of reach, often still with companions. Some called him a hero, others called him a nuisance and a bastard, but either way, he was the center of *someone's* attention. Their target, the knight Sir Tom Vincent Drake, clearly liked it that way.

The assassins, skilled though they were, had only ever gotten barely beyond the walls of the manor grounds. Each time they moved closer, something happened... like tonight – twice now.

Hooves charged down the street. Kye stopped in his tracks, and Niall still followed in his shadow. A group of armored knights arrived at the Drake Manor's entrance, dismounting their steeds. Two servants rushed over and threw open the metal gates with an ominous creak. The knights and servants argued about something to do with 'Sir Tom,' the assassins' target.

"We are fools and cowards," Niall declared from the darkness nearby. "We should just sneak in and kill him. It's been days, Kye – maybe even weeks; I lose track of time when I drink. The Messengers will send someone else, find us, and punish us for our incompetence. Our hesitation will be our doom."

Niall was a loyal member of the Silent Messengers, a mysterious group of assassins to which they both belonged – unfortunately. The Messengers had long ago taken in Kye when others would not, but his feelings about the situation were complicated. Kye looked over his shoulder at his partner, whose sour expression darkened the already deep creases of his face.

Kye shook his head. "We can't get near him—look at this. You wanna go over there and fight six knights? Even if we *did* win, we'd kill them in the middle of the street and then the rest of the city would be on us like hounds on a wolf."

"Then you would kill them, as a wolf does hounds."

"Yes, and what would *you* be doing?"

Niall didn't answer. Kye squinted at the colorful heraldry on the knights in question: yellow and blue, decorated with blue fishes. Fins adorned their metal armor. They were from the House of Marks, a family with which the Drakes often feuded.

"You've become too interested in your observations of the target," Niall pointed out, as if on cue. "We're meant to kill him, not study him."

"It's part of the process."

"But you must go through with it. You study enough to kill him, then you *kill* him. Or her. Or maybe even it, if it's an unborn child."

Kye's insides twisted. "I really don't want to hear about that."

"No? You've never had a target like that? I have been sent to kill an infant before, too. Sometimes some noble wants the firstborn dead." Niall shrugged. "Often it's the uncle. Easiest job you could ask for."

"People like you are why demons exist in the first place..." Kye muttered.

"What?"

"Nothing," Kye answered. He watched as the distant knights, still speaking loudly and with intent to wake the entire household, marched into the manor. Maybe Tom Drake had slept with the wrong woman again, as he was apparently wont to do. Whatever the case, their brief chance to get close to him – if it had ever really existed – was gone for the night.

Kye strode off down another street, leaving the manor behind. Niall's soft footsteps followed him.

"Where are we going?" he asked. "Don't you remember we have a job to do? A *late* job? And that the Messengers won't be happy with our performance?" Niall paused. "And do you plan to continue walking about the street looking the way you do?"

Kye said nothing. He knew he stood out in his gear, especially that vicious gauntlet he used so often. To compliment it, he wore on his left shoulder a single leather spaulder decorated in two upward-pointing metal spikes. A bandoleer of knives reaching across his chest completed his frightening attire. Niall, meanwhile, looked relatively unassuming in his travel cloak, even if it made him stand out when walking streets usually occupied by local nobility. As they left the wealthiest districts behind, however, such cloaked travelers drew fewer looks. After all, Illikon was a busy city and a port of trade, visited by all manner of folk, some from distant regions.

"Why am *I* the leader?" Kye retorted instead of addressing his outfit, even while he rested his metal-clawed hand on his sword-belt alongside the golden hilt of his curved-bladed *shamshir*, a Parsanshari weapon that Imperials often called a scimitar. Like so much of his outfit, his foreign and gilded sword also stood out. "*You* go kill him, if you're so capable. I'll back you up."

Not answering, Niall kept following. Kye returned to the open city streets but didn't walk near the lights. He stayed near the shadows, ready to disappear at a moment's notice.

"Then what are we doing instead?" Niall insisted, snatching for one of Kye's arms to make him stop, but Kye kept walking. "How are we still working toward our goal?"

"We'll get close to him a different way—"

A door flew open on the opposite side of the street. A skinny, haggard young man sprawled from it, bodily ejected from the building. He landed in a heap, putting his arms over his head and curling into the fetal position. Two larger figures stepped out after him, looming, hands curled into fists the size of bricks. Kye watched impassively, giving them a wide berth and hastening his gait. He wanted no part in whatever it was. Niall said nothing, not so much as glancing that way.

But as they left the scene behind, Kye still caught a few words. "We need something that will work by midnight tomorrow, or you're a dead man. The Watch is on us like flies, and we need to be gone. Understood?"

Kye shook his head. Corruption ran deep even in the most civilized and safest of places, and here he was a part of it. He frowned, but he didn't turn back.

"I am surprised to see criminals operating in this part of the city," Niall commented, keeping his voice low.

"Every part of a city has crime," replied Kye.

Niall scoffed. "You're wiser than I think sometimes."

"So are you, once in a while."

Again he scoffed, with more feeling this time, "It's rare for you, Kye. Like killing a watchman and compromising us not long after we arrived here. What if someone finds that body? And all because you like some stupid girl…"

Kye stopped, turning on his heel. Niall stopped too, instantly lifting his empty palms in fear. But Kye still pointed a long, metal-clawed left finger right at Niall's narrow chest.

"*Don't,*" he said, "call her stupid. And *you* just killed a guy too."

"Fine. Then tell me, where are we going when our target is behind us?"

Kye resumed leading. "To a tavern. I need to think, and I like doing that with food… and a drink."

"You are eager to drown in ale whatever otherworldly sorrows plague you, Kye, but you never actually seem to get drunk. Can… something like you actually *get* drunk? Does wasting coin on drink help your self-pity?"

"Will you leave me alone? I've got enough in my head without you trying to get in there too."

Niall chortled an unpleasant laugh. "It would be an interesting place. Perhaps I'd learn a thing or two about—"

"Niall? Shut up."

Finally, the other assassin fell silent. They continued undisturbed through the quiet, starlit Illikon. Kye slid into the shadows as a city watchman, clad in a chain shirt and a deep blue tabard decorated in the city's golden gryphon emblem, passed on the opposite side of the way. Niall's hand crept toward one of many daggers hidden on his person, but Kye pushed his arm away. The watchman gave them no trouble, moving on without a word.

Shortly thereafter, they reached a building with candles in the windows and noise leaking from an open doorway. Smells of roasted meat and finely-brewed ale reached Kye's nose, making his stomach growl and leading him inside.

The inn bustled with activity despite the late hour. Kye looked over the heads of assorted standing patrons, tall as he was. He spied the best path to a dark corner, exactly as Niall had predicted, and sat at a table away from the commotion. Niall followed close behind him as Kye's size parted a path through the crowd.

"Don't see our target in here, do you?" asked Niall, his dark eyes continuously darting everywhere.

"No," Kye replied, half in thought.

A barmaid came by. Kye ordered a drink, and Niall looked at him expectantly until Kye finally ordered one for him too. Once the barmaid left, Niall put on an ugly smile.

"I'm surprised you made it this far in the Messengers, Kye," he remarked. "You're so... what's the word? 'Nice?' I suppose that would work. Perhaps also 'gullible.' Easy to influence."

"No I'm not. It's your big brown... black... puppy-dog eyes," Kye replied wryly. "They're irresistible."

Niall's ugly smile dropped into a glare. "Do not tell me I'm cute."

Kye scoffed out a laugh. "Don't worry, I'm... I'm not gonna do that."

He looked around, searching for anything of interest. The crowd was surprisingly varied. Nobles mingled at certain tables, most staying apart from any common folk or strange travelers. One nobleman clad in a bright blue tunic caught Kye's eye – and the man stood, making a beeline for them.

"Who is he?" demanded Niall. Kye heard in his voice that he already plotted murder. He looked like a madman on the defensive, the whites of his eyes visible beneath furrowed brows.

"*Shh*," Kye hissed. "How should *I* know?"

The nobleman stopped at their table, resting his own tankard on it. The barmaid arrived at the same moment, dropping off their drinks, the fuller of which Niall immediately snatched. Their noble visitor not only wore a bright blue tunic, but it was pinned in place by a brooch of shining silver, depicting a trio of cresting waves. Kye didn't know what house that was, but he'd seen their target, Tom Drake, interact with people wearing such heraldry before... usually with a sorrowful air about him.

"Greetings," said the nobleman, plastering an amicable smile onto his good-looking face. His swept-back, platinum blond hair looked so perfect Kye almost thought it fake. "Haven't seen you two around before. Newcomers?"

Niall's already lined face darkened into an even worse scowl, and he didn't respond.

Kye cleared his throat and answered, managing a smile in return. "We are, actually. My name's Seth, and this is—"

"Do not tell him my name," Niall snapped.

Kye froze for a moment in aggravation and white-hot embarrassment, but the nobleman merely chuckled. "That's alright, friend," said the noble, "you needn't share it. It's nice to meet *you*, at least, Seth. You have a unique taste in attire. I don't see men dress in – well, in *spikes*. What brings such... flavorfully-clad folk to Illikon?"

Without intending it, Kye shifted in his seat. The nobleman's pale eyes drifted down Kye's side, landing on the beautiful, intricately-crafted scimitar he wore. Its golden hilt with its spiked finger-guard and crosspiece shone in the candlelight, and its dark leather sheath with elaborate designs was hardly subtle, either. Envy all but radiated from the man. Kye reached down with his gauntleted left hand and rested it protectively on his sword. The nobleman's eyes immediately cut back up to Kye's face.

"Just stopping by," Kye answered. Pointedly, he added, "I didn't actually get *your* name..."

"Oh. Gods, where are my manners?" the nobleman laughed it off as one might laugh at someone else's poor joke, and Kye narrowed his sky-blue eyes. "I am Faro Pelagius."

Niall coughed a chuckle past his tankard. "'Faro?'" he echoed incredulously.

Faro arched a faint eyebrow. "That *is* my name, yes. I am not however a '*pharaoh*,' like of Kemhet, if that's what you're wondering." Again he gave his laugh, which always sounded the same. It was meaningless. Kye heard no real mirth behind it.

"And what about you?" asked Kye. "Or do you always wander up to heavily-armed strangers and ask them their names?"

"A-ha! Good one, Seth. Good one... No, I only thought you looked rather lost, actually. I also thought you looked strikingly *noble*. Er – you, I mean, Seth."

"Thank you," Niall said. Faro looked confused at his genuineness. Niall's moist-lipped smile pulled his mouth wide, making him look like a toad with a dark mustache and goatee.

Kye said, "Thanks, but, um... I'm not really sure what that has to do with anything."

"It has plenty 'to do,' actually," replied Faro. "There's a banquet tomorrow evening in Castle Illikon. It won't be half as exciting as that banquet before Sir Tom and Sir Cassian nearly killed each other in their recent joust, but it should be entertaining, anyway..."

Kye's interest piqued at the mention of their target. "What happened at the joust?"

"You didn't hear? Sir Cassian nearly killed Sir Tom – it's a wonder he didn't, lancing him in the face like that. Then Sir Tom retaliated by nearly killing Sir Cassian in return." Faro laughed yet again. "It was quite a show. That Drake bastard went after him like a beast."

Niall's eyes cut Kye's way. Their gazes met briefly.

"That Drake bastard," Kye said, "being Sir Tom Drake, right?"

"Yes. He's a bastard son, if you didn't know. Half Nordling, to boot. The whole thing is a scandal, if you ask me – I don't know why he was ever allowed to become a knight, much less take a squire of his own..." Faro's voice drifted, and he shook his head. "Anyway, the banquet. No weapons are allowed, so you won't be able to carry these – sundry blades of yours."

Again, Faro glimpsed Kye's scimitar. Kye noticed, though he wasn't sure Faro meant him to, and his hand on his shamshir gripped a little tighter.

"Right," Kye said blandly.

"All the nobility are invited, as are many travelers, even some only passing through. Seeing as I... recently *lost* my nephew and have no sons to parade about, I cannot be charitable and bring them, so I thought I'd be charitable by inviting someone else instead. You two look like just the men I would love to see shaking up such a banquet." Faro's fake smile returned in a flash. "What do you say? I'd love to hear your stories."

"So you are inviting us to get back at some other noble who wronged you," Niall said. "Is that it?"

Faro screwed up his brow. After a moment, he replied, "Something like that, friend. You catch on quick."

Niall laughed – probably the first real laugh of the conversation. "I like you. We will attend the banquet. Isn't that right, 'Seth?'"

Kye's left hand wandered back up to the table, where he absently scratched a line in the wood with a long, metal claw. "Yeah – sure, we'll come. Why not, I guess."

Faro clapped his hands together. "*Wonderful.* I assume you have something to wear or can acquire it – you can't walk in there looking like *that*. You'll be my personal guests of honor. Anyway, see you then."

With that, the nobleman swept away as suddenly as he'd appeared, returning to a table of men dressed like him and leaving the pair of darkly-clad warriors behind. Niall laughed again, but Kye bit his lip at the strange symbols he'd absently etched into the wooden table. He scratched them out in a hurry as the barmaid returned, dropping off their food.

"What a rich fool," Niall remarked while Kye dug into his plate. "Inviting smelly strangers to a banquet just because some other noble angered him. It's incredible. I wish I was a noble and played such games."

"You'd be good at it. And *I'm* not smelly. You're the one who apparently hates baths."

"They're a waste of time only women should indulge in. Like this banquet will be, if we spend too long there."

"Actually, it might be the breakthrough we need. Tom Drake might be there."

Niall hummed thoughtfully, taking another swig of ale.

"But," Kye continued, "if that Faro guy thinks he can buy my scimitar, he's in for a disappointment."

"Did he mention that?"

"He kept staring."

"I see. Well, if he does make you an offer, you can get another sword. We can even take some months and go all the blasted way to Parsanshar and get you another shamshir, if you love them so much. I'd take his gold."

"I'm sure you would, Niall, but it's personal." Kye scooted his own tankard closer. "I don't like the way he looked at it..."

"Sometimes men look at each other's swords."

Kye paused in the middle of guzzling his tankard, staring past the rim of his cup at Niall.

A beat passed.

"That is not what I meant," Niall said.

"I hope not, or I *know* I'm not going," Kye muttered, setting his drained tankard down. Niall eyed it.

"You remind me of a Legionary, wolfing down your food like that. Were you in some military or another?"

"No, I was just starved my whole life." Kye hesitated; he hated answering questions so reflexively. "I mean... um. None of your business."

Niall shook his head. "You're an odd one."

"Yeah, you've mentioned that about a dozen times since we first got partnered up."

"I cannot stop wondering about you. I know what you—"

Kye sat up straighter – so straight he loomed over not only the table but Niall as well, his broad shoulders casting a shadow on his fellow assassin. Niall snapped his jaws shut.

A moment later, however, Niall reluctantly finished, "What is it, then? Your sword. Some kind of historical weapon? Family heirloom?"

"No one here would know," Kye answered, his tone dark and uncharacteristically terse. He settled back into his seat.

"They wouldn't? Is it..." Niall's mouth fell open. "Is it some kind of accursed artifact? Is it *magic?*"

"You wanna say that any louder? Stop asking so many questions. You weren't like this when we were traveling. You didn't even say two words."

"I do not like talking when traveling, but now I'm drinking. It's very different. Anyway, I like knowing about people – learning secrets." His broad smile returned, lifting his patchy mustache. "Always good to know others' secrets."

Kye shook his head, saying, "You're a horrible person."

Niall kept smiling. After rolling his eyes, Kye reached across the table, grabbed Niall's drink, and drained its contents.

After finishing their meals, the two departed the inn and found even quieter streets than before. Night settled well over the city of Illikon. Pulling in a deep breath of the cool air, Kye tasted the coming winter. His luck being what it was, of course he'd received an assignment in the Northwestern Empire on the cusp of the coldest time of year. He hated cold.

"These Northmen and their Northwestern kin are all mad," said Niall as they set off. "Rumors of war circulate everywhere. Half the tavern was talking about it. Who goes to war in winter?"

"Northmen, I guess," Kye answered. "The crazy ones, anyway."

"And the insane Imperial Heartlanders looking for any excuse to retaliate, perhaps. I've heard tell the Frost Ravens are leading the charge... We need to kill that knight and get out of here before the gates are so heavily guarded even *we* cannot escape."

But Niall's words were lost on him. Kye heard a woman's frantic voice begging for help. Though he knew he shouldn't have, Kye stopped. Niall halted behind him, narrowing his eyes.

"What?" he snapped, hearing nothing.

Kye only lifted a single long, metal claw on his left hand, quieting his partner. Niall scowled. Without explanation, Kye slipped through an alley and down another street, peering out into a lane – one that wouldn't lead them to the shoddy inn where they'd been spending their nights. A loud sigh erupted behind him: Niall's way of pointing out the divergence from their path. Kye ignored him.

In the doorway of her home, a robust, heavy-set Northwoman with long blond hair spoke to a pair of men in chain shirts. Sparse candlelight from within the house shone on their chests, showing the golden gryphon on their blue tabards. Watchmen of Illikon...

Desperation filled the woman's voice. "She's missing – my little girl, someone took her! You have to do *something!*"

"Calm down," said a watchman. "Tell us what happened."

"I— I don't know! She was right beside me, and when I turned for only a moment, she was gone! I thought she'd only run ahead, but she isn't inside – you *must* help me find her! A little girl alone this time of night!?"

"When was the last time you saw her? Minutes ago, an hour...?"

"*Kye,*" Niall hissed, grabbing one of Kye's muscle-bound bare arms. He tugged it so sharply that Kye faced him. "I don't know why you care about this, but this is not our *mission*. We need clothing for that banquet."

Kye jerked his arm from Niall's grip, but he didn't protest. Blocking out the mother's frantic words, he resumed the trek to Illikon's slums.

Kye said, "It's the middle of the night. We can't buy anything right now. Do we have enough money, anyway? Won't it be expensive? I've never bought anything like that before."

"We have enough. If *you* don't, though, I'm not covering for you."

Kye sighed.

"I'll be at the Donkey," said Niall. He meant the Flogged Donkey inn and tavern, where he and Kye were staying. Kye didn't care for it, but at least it was affordable and not frequented by knights or even watchmen... except one watchman friend of Tom Drake's who liked to drink there, but he paid them no heed.

"And I'll go find a shop that sells tunics," Kye replied, "and do all the work."

"Yes. I enjoy our relationship. I'm hoping you'll learn from it."

Kye didn't comment.

Niall went on, "This is why I'd make an excellent nobleman. I know how to command and use others, like that nobleman tonight wants to use us to make some sort of point."

"'Command?'" Kye echoed incredulously. "You were the one following *me* earlier."

"One must sometimes feign following in order to lead. If you push too hard, always lead and command, then your victim becomes aware. The real trick is making sure he never realizes it. Your desires must become his – but *he* must think the desires wholly his own. You see?"

Kye rubbed the back of his neck with his right hand. "That's *really* twisted. I hate it."

Niall smiled an ugly smile. "Thank you. Manipulation is an art. And, of course, there's the simple fact that the leader will be blamed, attacked, or even killed before the follower. Then the follower can escape."

"Great. That ale is helping me learn a lot about you."

Prompted, Niall fell silent. A glare crawled over Kye's skin like ants, and he regarded a sneering Niall.

"What'd I do *now?*" Kye asked, throwing his hands out.

"You're nervous again. You are always nervous. It's a terrible trait. Fix it."

"So is that supposed to be my desire or yours?" Kye retorted.

Niall looked ready to slap him.

"And what makes you think I'm nervous, anyway?" he added, mustering a decent amount of outrage. He kept rubbing the back of his neck. Niall shook his head.

"Go scout, Kye. I'll be drinking."

They parted ways, disappearing into the night.

Purchasing suitable clothing was easy enough, and on the day of the banquet, Kye and Niall strode through Illikon clad in relative finery. Kye's tunic was bright golden-yellow, Niall's toga white with a rusty brown-red sash. Kye readjusted his attire self-consciously, knowing it showed off his physique. Niall, meanwhile, didn't look bothered. He also didn't look good.

Kye felt naked without his knives... and especially without his scimitar. More than once, he reflexively attempted resting his left hand on its hilt at his hip, only to find it missing. At least he didn't have to concern himself with weapons right now – in theory, anyway. All that concerned him was maintaining his focus.

When they neared Castle Illikon, however, they found an army.

Imperial knights marched down the main road leading directly from Illikon's eastern gates to the castle. Every single one rode on horseback – and every single one was suited for battle, not ceremony. Kye stopped abruptly on the side of the street with so many other bystanders, blinking in confusion, towering in the crowd.

"What the hell is this?" said Niall.

"Didn't you hear?" asked a woman nearby; people seemed more inclined to speak with them when they wore ordinary clothing instead of armor and weapons like a pair of killers. "They're leaving for Northrim. Things have gotten bad up there, they say." She shook her head. "I fear war will soon be upon us."

"It'll be a quick one," another bystander remarked. "The Empire's crushed barbarian tribes countless times."

"I've heard the barbarians are united now. Seems like a bunch of nonsense. I'm not sure what to believe anymore."

Niall added nothing, looking back at the knights. He said only, "This is our luck."

"You can say that again," Kye replied almost distantly, because he saw who led the army.

Heading the knights from across the Northwestern Empire rode their target, Sir Tom Drake, clad in his steel muscle cuirass decorated in bright red dragons and the golden crown of Achaea. His helmet also was in the style of an Old Achaean hoplite but covered in dragon motifs, his nose-guard a dragon head, topped in a tall and proud horsehair crest of bright blood red running from his forehead to the back of his skull. The long tail of it hung down his neck. He stood out even among the other knights, given his crest and bare, muscular arms. He looked like some old Achaean hero from the Empire's Golden Age.

The dragon knight rode his horse under Illikon's gatehouse, disappearing onto the open, sprawling plains of golden grass surrounding the city. Kye sensed Niall's growing despair before he even spoke. His partner turned in a circle and looked in every direction before finally glaring Kye accusingly in the face.

"*Now* what do we do?" Niall hissed.

Kye didn't answer at first. He watched the army go, more men than easily countable following Drake's lead...

"This is *your* fault," Niall said, jabbing a finger into Kye's side with enough force to drive a dagger. "You've been distracted this entire time by something or another and you've let him *escape*."

"He didn't 'escape,'" Kye retorted immediately. "He's—right there. He's coming back. And anyway, if he doesn't, then... I guess it's taken care of."

Niall scoffed. "What of this banquet, then? Do we still go? What even is the point now?"

"To learn things. We rub elbows with these nobles Drake is a part of, and maybe we can do something to get closer to him when he comes back. It's not like we've been able to get close enough to kill him before now, anyway."

Unconvinced, Niall only snorted. Kye resisted informing him how often he did that. Navigating the streets as the rest of the knight army departed the city, Kye led them to Castle Illikon, following a small train of nobles heading that way. The drawbridge lay at rest, allowing them passage into the vast castle grounds. Horses tended by stable-hands stood about on the grass. Many steeds wore colorful banners of different noble houses, dotting the green plain with bright hues of red, blue, yellow, more green, and silver, among others. Kye didn't recognize many family sigils, but he knew a few from his time spent figuring out how to discreetly kill Drake.

Men and women in fine togas, stolas, and tunics of assorted designs and colors filed into Castle Illikon. A few wore more unusual attire, white and with even more skin revealed, along with intricate jewelry of gold and azure. They were from the nigh-impossibly distant land of Kemhet, far to the south.

"Real Kemhetis? Here?" Niall said in surprise. The assassins had posed as travelers from Kemhet when they'd first entered Illikon. Foreign visitors from far distant lands frequented Illikon more often than they'd realized.

Kye followed the crowd until they found themselves in a feast hall, where the many guests took seats at a great table of dark wood. Others remained standing, several with goblets in hand, and chattered about gossip, news, and diplomatic matters. If Kye fit in anywhere, he thought, this scene was surely the opposite.

Then he saw a huge problem only a few feet away.

Kye recognized a few warriors among the nobility, easily spotted either by their scars or because they wore ceremonial armor in place of usual noble attire. One such warrior was a knight conversing with a Kemheti – and, emblazoned in red and gold on the knight's tabard, was the four-pointed star of the goddess Astra Aeterna.

Kye swallowed. The cult of Astra Aeterna, The Eternal Star, had only risen to prominence in Achaea recently. A few decades ago, an Emperor named Antares had declared himself an Astra worshiper and put her star on the Imperial crown. Since then, knightly orders had arisen in her service, despite the goddess rarely interacting directly with Men, according to her followers.

The knight in question looked like a member of one such order. Specifically, one called the Knights Templar, who served as intermediaries among the many Olympian temples in the Achaean Empire. Rigid in their duty, obscenely rich, and accepting only the noblest of noble, the Knights Templar not only used their worship of Astra to remain impartial among the politics of the Olympian-worshipers... they also used their holy light to hunt and banish all evil. Though any truly unholy evil crossing over into the realm of Men was beyond rare, should anyone bear witness to such a thing, the Knights Templar answered the call to slay it.

Blood drained from Kye's face. What was one of them doing *here?* Illikon had no Templar presence...

"Food," Niall astutely observed aloud, pointing at a table of finger-food set out as appetizers before the feast. "I'm going to go get some."

"Wait," Kye said, grabbing his shoulder. "Could you at least *try* to have manners?"

"Why? That Faro man invited us because we look like we have none, did he not?" He chortled. "Well, me, at least. Apparently *you're* quite the pretty-boy."

Kye rolled his eyes. "All I'm saying is, don't draw too much attention, okay?" His attention flicked to the man wearing the star of Astra again. "Especially not from him."

Niall followed his eyes, his mouth forming a perfect 'O' afterward. "I see. It's no concern of *mine*, but since we're partners..." he allowed a pause before finishing, "I'll do as I already planned and go eat food. How does that sound?"

He freed himself from Kye's grip so hard several people nearby looked over in alarm, perhaps expecting a brawl breaking out. Kye straightened his tunic again and, stealing a final look at the knight of Astra, followed Niall.

Along the way, Kye kept his ears open for any interesting conversations. Someone excitedly mentioned a *thalamegos*, which Kye figured or at least hoped was a ship, in the waters off the coast of Illikon. It sounded like a highly unusual occurrence. He also heard discussions about the weather and a storm, and several people talked about the visitors from Kemhet, seemingly connected with said '*thalamegos.*' More gossip that largely flew over his head wasted away his attention span. By the time he neared the food table, Kye had stopped listening. He snatched a goblet of wine—

"Earl Warren Drake," someone behind Kye said, "did your son not just ride to war?"

Kye nearly choked. He resisted looking behind him at the father of his target. During their time studying Tom Drake, both he and Niall had become familiar with the family patron, but never had Kye been this close to him before. He saw in his mind's eye Earl Warren in his red and gold tunic adorned with dragon sigils and motifs, yet he focused only on the food in front of him, remaining casual.

"There is no 'war,'" answered a deep voice – Warren Drake, Tom's father.

"Then why would Illikon march an army of so many knights out the front gates – heading north?"

"I do not participate in gossip, and military affairs are not the concern of merchant lords. If you wish to discuss rumors, you'd be better served seeking Earl Cassius and his wine-soaked son."

Footsteps walked away; Kye assumed Warren had left. Glancing at Niall, Kye received a subtle nod of confirmation from his partner. Finally, Kye turned – and saw Faro standing right behind him. He nearly started.

"You two did make it, after all," Faro declared with one of his bland chuckles. "How are you enjoying the banquet?"

"Not really used to this stuff," Kye replied reluctantly.

"Indeed? I would've thought such affairs could provide ample entertainment for uncommon travelers, witnessing Illikon's glory..."

In the corner of his eye, Kye noticed the holy knight's colorful tabard— he was coming their way. Every hair on the back of Kye's neck stood on end. A chill crawled across his skin. He wanted to run.

"Lord Faro," the holy knight said, "I must speak with you."

Kye knew a good ounce of color drained from his face, leaving him feeling cold, but he resisted looking at the Templar. He kept his gaze on Faro and forced as natural an expression as he could.

"I'm currently speaking with some friends," Faro shot back, hostile. Kye swallowed so loudly it sounded comical.

"That's alright," Kye nearly blurted. "We'll be around."

Faro glared at him as if he'd expected Kye to back him up somehow. Kye plastered on a nervous, half-cocked smile.

The holy knight said again, "Lord Faro."

"*Fine,*" he spat. Faro paused, inhaled, and corrected calmly, "Fine. I shall speak with you again soon, then, Seth." He allowed the Templar to lead him off, but Kye heard Faro say, "I already saw you interrogating another of my friends, one who traveled far to meet me. What exactly is your intent, knight?"

Kye waited until they left. Relief crashed into him like the surf against Illikon's rocky coast. Not wasting a moment, he gripped Niall's nearest arm, hauling him back toward the door. Niall sputtered in outrage.

"What— what are you *doing?*"

"We're leaving," Kye said flatly.

"Why? Because you are a coward?"

"*No*, because I don't want to die horribly."

"That's called cowardice."

"You'd know, wouldn't you?"

Kye kept going. He glanced back at the holy knight, whose back was turned. Faro stared the Templar in the face, brow furrowed. Though Kye wondered why a Templar would irritate another noble so much, he didn't care. Probably nothing but convoluted noble politics, anyway.

No one stopped them. Despite his claims, Niall followed Kye without complaint, so he released his arm. Kye rounded the corner, now but a few steps away from freedom...

And he ran right into a nobleman. Kye nearly barreled the man straight into the ground in his haste, but the noble caught himself on sturdy legs. Kye stumbled back and immediately showed his hands.

"Whoa, sorry," he blurted, "I was just—"

Earl Warren Drake regarded him, his deep blue eyes judging in silence. A knot formed in Kye's throat and silenced him. Warren, however, merely straightened himself and fixed the askew golden amulet around his neck, one depicting the family's rearing heraldic dragon. Kye had seen Tom Drake wearing an amulet exactly the same but of silver.

"It's alright," said Warren. He paused. "You must be foreign. I don't recognize you. Did you come on that *thalamegos?*"

"Uhhh," Kye began, feeling uniquely stupid. Niall appeared alongside him and butted in.

"No," said Niall. "We came from the land, not the sea. We are not that rich."

Warren arched a brow. "I see." He glanced them up and down. Kye's skin crawled; Warren's attention lingered on him in particular. "I feel I've seen you before..."

"Really?" Kye laughed it off, not sure it was his best effort. "I'm nobody."

Warren looked unconvinced, but he shrugged. "Whoever you are, you seem to be in quite the hurry to leave. I'll not take any more of your time. Good day."

With that, Earl Warren Drake swept off, his one-shouldered red cape trailing behind him. Kye sighed so heavily in relief his shoulders sagged. Niall, however, loudly sucked his teeth and took a few steps back, watching Warren rejoin the banquet.

"Now the father knows what we look like," Niall said darkly.

"Who cares?" replied Kye, resuming his walk. "The whole idea of being assassins is that we aren't seen when we do our job. And we aren't after him."

"You make good points. Far better than you usually make, in fact."

"Have you ever given a real compliment in your life?"

"No."

They passed by many beautifully-clad Illikon royal guards and watchmen on their way out. Worry and fear were plain on the faces of everyone Kye passed. Even Warren had the same air about him, Kye thought, albeit subtler. The war *was* about to start – everyone in Illikon feared it... and everyone knew it, too, whether they admitted it or not.

"We really need to do our job and get out of here," Kye muttered.

"That's what I've been telling you."

"At least we didn't have to go all the way to Rimegard with the others..."

Niall choked out a harsh chortle. "Yes, that'd be rich. I'd be surprised if that place hasn't already fallen to the barbarians. Where are we going now?"

"I," replied Kye, "am going back to the inn and getting my *stuff*. I need my weapons."

"Planning to murder another watchman?" Niall asked coyly.

Kye threw him a sharp look. "I dunno. Are *you* planning to murder another random civilian?"

Niall's expression didn't change.

Kye finished, "No, I'm not. I just I want my sword. I'd like my daggers too, but I need my sword."

Kye offered no further justification, heading straight out the castle gate and through the grounds, taking the quickest path back to their shoddy room in the Flogged Donkey.

When he arrived at their room, Kye knew something was wrong.

A sixth sense warned him before he even opened the door – and though nothing immediately appeared out of place, Kye's eyes locked on the shoddy bed that was too small for him. Before leaving for the banquet, he'd placed his scimitar in its sheath underneath it, hidden beneath some random clothing.

The clothing had been pushed aside. His sword was gone.

Kye froze in the doorway, his mighty frame silhouetted in the light. He set his jaw. Behind him, Niall ducked beneath his arm, peering at whatever drew his stare.

"I'm such an idiot..." Kye groaned.

Niall cut his eyes up at him. "I've pointed this out many times," he said, pushing past Kye. He went to his own possessions, rifled through them, and barked a triumphant laugh. "They took none of *my* things."

Looking through his own and discovering nothing else missing, Kye said, "That's because nothing else here is really all that valuable."

"And that strange scimitar of yours *is*."

Kye hesitated. But he answered firmly, "Yes."

"Well that's a shame, but it's nothing to fret over. We can get you a new weapon."

Surging to his feet, desperate frustration overtaking him, Kye inspected the nearby window – clearly how the thief had broken in – and shook his head. "I'm getting it back."

"Tell me you're joking."

Kye's voice held more determination than it had during his entire stay in Illikon. "No. I'm getting it back, Niall. Tom Drake isn't even here right now anyway – we don't *have* a target."

Niall threw his things down like a child having a tantrum. "Why do you care so much about that blasted sword? It's *another* distraction! Is it pride? Is it because you're too good to use an ordinary weapon like the rest of us?"

"This isn't about pride," Kye answered. His tone, for once, silenced his partner. "That ridiculous nobleman, Faro, couldn't take his eyes off it. He even commented on it, indirectly or not. And he *knew* I wouldn't have it with me for that stupid useless banquet... He must've hired somebody to steal it for him while we weren't here." Kye rubbed the long, metal claws of his left gauntlet together, though they made almost no sound when he did. Niall watched, one eye twitching; he knew only dark magic could silence metal so. "I'm going to Faro's place."

"You what?" Niall coughed a guttural laugh, which gurgled with phlegm. Kye grimaced at the sound. "You are mad. I considered us lucky that our target spends almost no time in his family's distant castle, fortified as it must be – but we can scarcely get near the Drake manor here in Illikon, either. And now you want to break into a *different* one?"

"The Pelagius family isn't quite as rich as the Drakes. We can do it."

Niall paused and thought about that. His pensiveness lasted only a moment before he declared, "Alright, I'll come."

Kye snorted. "Yeah, I thought so. Take whatever you want while we're there; I don't care. I'm just getting my sword... but I also wanna know what some Illikon nobleman could possibly want with it. Or how he'd know anything *about* it."

"Why *would* someone want it?"

If nothing else, Kye owed Niall that much. Reluctantly, he looked his partner in the face again. For once, Niall waited, not pressuring him. Kye took a deep breath before giving his honest answer.

"Because it wasn't forged here by some mortal hammer and anvil. It was shaped in the Underworld by the ancient demon lord Akhoman, King of All Agonies, a fallen god... and he made it for me."

Niall asked no more questions, nor did he protest. They set out that evening, shortly before the *lanternarii* would light every candle in the posts along the richer city streets. Kye hastened for the Monument District, where most of the nobility had their manors within Illikon's city limits. Hopefully, Faro was still there and hadn't already departed for whatever outlying land he or his family owned...

Following directions from a passer-by, Kye once again led the way. Niall trailed several feet behind, maintaining his distance. Kye didn't bother keeping an eye on him, using the sound of his footfalls, quiet though they were, to know his partner was still with him.

Among the other beautiful homes in the Monument District, the Pelagius family manor appeared outright unassuming. Anyone of common blood living in such a spacious home would feel like a king, but compared to the estates of greater families, it looked like a simple, two-story building with only a handful of rooms. Kye wondered if they even had any servants... maybe one or two, at best.

As they neared, Kye nimbly leapt up onto one of the lampposts outside, swiping the candle from it with a reach of his long arm. He did the same with the next light. Niall watched him, perplexed, following when Kye slipped into a nearby alley.

"What are you doing?" demanded Niall, sounding as outraged as usual.

"Buying us a little extra time," Kye replied, handing Niall the candles. He stuffed them into his sling-bag like a packrat.

An hour passed, then an hour and a half – and Kye watched a lanternarius arrive, lifting a flame on a pole toward the waiting candle in the lamppost, as he had for all the others. Finding no candle, however, he paused and sighed. He checked the next light before leaving. Newly lit light-posts now staved off the night, save for around the home of Faro Pelagius. Kye considered himself lucky this region of the city used candles instead of oil lamps. They wouldn't have been so easy to remove.

"You're smarter than I thought," Niall scoffed.

"Thanks. I think?"

Kye, however, didn't return to the main street. He carefully climbed a few feet up the side of the Pelagius home, finding handholds with his right and making sturdier ones with his left. Kye reached a window, tugging on the sill before deeming it safe and using it to hoist himself higher.

Crime in the Monument District of Illikon was nearly unheard of, but watchmen still patrolled here. Given the war close on the horizon, Kye hoped the night watch had their hands full with refugees and other assorted restlessness... but he heard voices and footsteps on the street, coming his way.

Niall hissed a warning up at him. Kye moved quickly.

Sliding the glass pane from its housing, Kye looked down at Niall, who waited below. He dropped the pane – and Niall caught it perfectly, gently propping it against the building. Kye tested the interior shutters but found them locked. Sliding the tip of a long claw between them, he easily pushed the latch out of place. It was hardly very sturdy, especially against his gauntlet.

He slid the shutters open, motioning down to Niall before slipping inside. A hall stretched before him, relatively undecorated; surprisingly so, for a noble family. Two more shuttered windows let in no light, and Kye waited a moment, his sensitive eyes quickly adjusting to the semidarkness. On his right was a closed door marked with a three-pronged trident, the favored holy symbol of Poseidon. Other ritual items lay around its base like some kind of shrine. Kye shivered, giving the door a wide berth.

Voices drifted from the stairwell at the far end of the hall behind him. They sounded increasingly agitated. Hopefully whatever was happening would distract the servants, if there were any...

Niall soon joined him, carefully sliding the window shut behind them. Only one door in the hall stood ajar. Kye approached it gingerly, peering through the crack and keeping his ears open. It seemed unoccupied, so he slowly entered the chamber.

He stepped into a fairly sizable room, a combination of a bedroom and study, with yet another shuttered window. An ajar door led to a small washroom, and there were other furniture and personal items, but Kye took an interest in the writing desk directly opposite of the door. He approached and glanced it over, eyes alighting on a pile of parchments – and something odder resting beside them.

It was like a soft sculpture. It resembled a cat, if crudely rendered. Unfamiliar with the specifics of mortal materials, Kye didn't know what it was made of, but it was soft and fluffy, colored saffron – a yellow-gold; Kye always heard it likened to the orange fruits of Parsanshar – with red stripes sewn in, crafted from scraps of nobles' colorful tunics. Frowning thoughtfully, Kye picked up the little crude plush cat, its face of black button eyes and a crookedly-sewn nose staring back at him. Something about it felt wrong, even sad, though Kye couldn't place exactly why.

"What is that?" asked Niall in a harsh whisper, side-eying him.

"A child's toy, I guess," Kye replied quietly. "But Faro said he didn't have any offspring. Maybe someone else in the house does."

Niall went to the writing desk, pawing through a few parchments. "Or maybe not. This does seem to be *his* room, judging by the address on the letters." He paused. "Nyx's mercy."

"What?"

Picking up the letter, Niall said, "I needn't know much of nobility trying to write in code to decipher this. They're talking about kidnappings. Trafficking. Or attempted ones, at least. I knew a smuggler once who used the same language to discuss cases with his clients. He worked with the Trade Guild. By that I mean, *the* Trade Guild. Imperials should perhaps vary their methods..."

"Kidnapping? For what?"

"Whoever Faro is corresponding with, he mentions needing an artifact of great power."

Kye scowled. "Fang..."

"What?"

"My sword."

"Your sword has a name? And it's named 'Fang?'"

Hesitantly, Kye answered, "That's what *I* called it. I'm not saying its real name, not in this world, and not so near those holy symbols outside."

Niall grunted, dropping the parchment and looking elsewhere. Kye, meanwhile, stuffed the plush animal in his belt. It looked ridiculous, carried at his hip where he generally kept his *shamshir.* Niall blinked at him in disbelief.

"You cannot be serious," he said. "What's your interest in that thing?"

"I don't know yet, it just bothers me," Kye answered. "But I know it can't belong to Faro. If they kidnapped somebody, it probably belongs to someone else's child, so I don't like it being here."

"Now you're going to concern yourself with children or the imagined feelings of toys? Are you a child, yourself?"

"I wasn't born in this world of color and pretty little animals and growing things like *you* were," Kye retorted, throwing out his gauntleted hand. "It's not *my* fault you take all this for granted."

"Take *what* for granted?" asked Niall, not looking at him. He paid more heed to a thick, old tome bound in black leather he found beneath the pillow of Faro's bed, which he of course was busy ransacking. He cracked the book open before adding, "Silly little toys of cats? Yes, I'm so thankful for those."

"Nevermind," Kye muttered, picking up a parchment set out on the writing desk like something recently penned.

"Your fascination with this realm is very amusing, Kye, but you must leave it behind at some point and focus on your..." his voice drifted, "work..." He suddenly looked up at Kye again, holding aloft the dark tome. "Is this what you really look like?"

Kye's nerves shattered. He wheeled and saw Niall presenting an illumination of Akhoman, the most ancient of all demon lords. It was a crude and speculative depiction, yet it was near enough to the truth that it made Kye blanch. Two large arms and two smaller arms, all bearing three clawed fingers... four horns, great spreading wings, a long tail ending in a spearhead, and they even roughly captured his toothy, fanged head, which mortals likened to a canine skull—

"This face... it nearly reminds me of an illumination I saw once – of a werewolf. But this is a demon," Niall added. His voice dripped with fear. His eyes avoided Kye's own. "I've never heard of such things."

"And *I've* never seen a werewolf," Kye answered, terse. "I don't know a lot about them."

"You don't want to. Trust me. I never have seen one either, or I assume I'd be dead, from the stories I've heard. They wear the guises of men... also not unlike you."

Kye's nostrils flared. Niall didn't see it.

"Though those beasts must shed their false skins under the moon's light, and *you*—"

Lunging, Kye slammed the book shut on Niall's fingers. Niall hissed and swore.

"Okay," said Kye acidly, "that's enough about your scary mortal fairytales. I don't have anything to do with the werewolf curse, neither does Akhoman, and what Akhoman might or might not look like isn't any of your concern. Let's focus. Like why does Faro have a *tome about demons?* Imperials don't exactly copy those."

With a snort, Niall muttered, "Saying we need to focus is rich coming from you, particularly with that silly toy in your belt."

Kye read the parchment in his hand, not listening. It too was a letter, and it spoke of something called a *thalamegos*. The thing he'd kept hearing about at the party... The great ship.

"What even is a *thalamegos?*" asked Kye.

"A pleasure barge, essentially. Like that one anchored off the coast of Illikon as we speak, the one people at the banquet couldn't shut up about. They are impossibly expensive and difficult to manage. It's so large it can't dock here in the city. Why? Does Faro own it? I thought most or all of them were from the Heartland and Kemhet. Gods, that lying miser must be richer than a dragon..."

Kye didn't point out the envy in Niall's voice. "Yeah, well, we need to get to it somehow. Faro is headed there tonight –

he must've already left. He wrote he has 'the artifact,' and that—"

The letter ended mid-hand. Realization pulled Kye's shoulders taut.

He suddenly grabbed Niall with his enormous left gauntlet, dragging his partner to the nearby washroom door. Niall struggled in protest, spitting some choice swears, but he couldn't escape Kye's grip. Kye shoved Niall inside and then squeezed in after him, pushing the door almost entirely shut. The washroom was even smaller than Kye thought at first glance. Small spaces irritated him, and Niall being there made it so much worse.

"Why in Hades are we hiding in a private lavatorium like a pair of weeping women?" Niall snapped, shoving up uncomfortably close beside him and peering out at the empty bedroom.

"Faro didn't finish his letter," Kye answered, keeping his voice low. "Somebody interrupted him but he didn't even put it away, so he left in a hurry. I'm pretty sure somebody's looking for him, and I bet they're the ones downstairs right now. I'm surprised they didn't already walk in on us..."

Niall snorted again. "So, we'll kill them."

"What'd I say about not leaving a trail of bodies?"

"Indeed, too late; you already started it."

"Nobody *found* him, and I didn't *mean* to do it," Kye hissed defensively.

"Shush," Niall ordered. Kye angrily snapped his jaws shut. Niall was right – footsteps approached from the hall outside, bringing voices with them.

"...the day the Empire even suspects its own and its allies," an accented voice finished in a biting tone.

"I needn't explain myself to you," replied a man with a voice like stone. Kye thought he recognized it.

"You certainly haven't. Your accusations are ridiculous, and what you are doing is outside the jurisdiction of your order."

The door to Faro's room swung open. In stepped a lavishly-dressed man from Kemhet, one Kye had seen at the banquet. He wore a deep scowl, his pale eyes darting over the room and its contents in a hurry, as though wondering what he should put away. And the holy knight, also from the banquet, followed him.

Kye's throat tightened.

"You and Faro may take that up with the master of my chapter," said the Knight Templar.

The Kemheti barked a laugh. "And where is that? All the way in Caltha, or do you have no chapter *that* far north, either? Vyzigord, perhaps, or did that Duke run you out in favor of his own order? I know you knights enjoy butting heads."

"You ask many questions I will not answer. Each word you speak, however, tells me more of your guilt."

The Kemheti sneered, but Kye noted the way he went to the writing desk and backed into it, hands behind him. His wandering fingers deftly found the unfinished letter, without looking, and stuffed it into the backside of his garments. Niall exhaled a scarcely suppressed, nasally laugh. Feeling Niall's breath, confined as they were, made Kye wonder if he could simply tear down the walls for immediate escape.

"And why do you assume I'm guilty?" asked the Kemheti. "Why do you assume Faro, a prestigious noble, uncle of a boy who was fated to become a knight of Illikon, is also guilty?

You realize that of which you accuse him is the same thing that killed his own nephew – cut him down in his squirehood."

"I am aware," the Templar answered, his steely gaze scanning the room. "That is precisely what might fascinate him into such crimes."

"Madness," the Kemheti declared. "I remind you again that such darkness killed young Radek. Why would that lead a man to fascination?"

But the knight didn't respond. He didn't move. His eyes were locked directly on the door to the washroom. Kye's heart pumped ice.

The Knight Templar saw them.

"Go— go, go!" Kye nearly shouted, shoving Niall out the door. He staggered from the washroom face-first, catching himself and darting for the exit. Kye went on his heels, straight into the hall, not looking back.

"Thieves!" cried the Kemheti man. "After them!"

"They are no common thieves," Kye heard the knight say, his words accentuated by the ring of steel leaving its sheath— "There is too great an evil about them."

"Niall, *run faster!*" Kye urged, voice cracking from terror. Niall took the approaching corner first, barreling at such speed he grabbed the wall and spun around it to make the turn. Kye did the same, the claws of his gauntlet leaving ruts in the wood. They faced yet another hall – but it opened at the far end into a staircase leading down. The exit.

"Run where!?" Niall barked back. "You were too incompetent to plan an escape!"

"That guy's a knight, I bet he had a horse – we'll take that, now go!"

"Both of us on *one* horse!?"

"Ahriman's breath, who cares, just keep running!"

Footsteps thundered close behind, the loud pounding of the knight's boots. A chill ran up Kye's neck, but he dared not risk looking back. He passed a stand holding a bust – and reached out, digging his claws in, knocking it to the floor in his wake. An even louder crash followed when the knight tripped over it.

They neared the exit— Niall took off down the stairs while Kye leapt and cleared both railing and banister, landing heavily but gracefully. Niall skidded to a stop scarcely before crashing into him, and Kye threw himself out the front door.

Cold night air hit him in the face. Still the two candle-posts outside the manor remained unlit, giving them the advantage of darkness. A horse hitched nearby whinnied at the sight of them, while another steed beside it remained calmer. But two horses meant...

Two knights.

Something swung at Niall's skull. He ducked narrowly in time. The mace's head grazed Kye's left arm instead, scraping his segmented armor there.

Immediately, Kye drew a dagger from the belt over his chest and lunged at the second Knight Templar. The bodkin point drove neatly through the knight's tabard and mail shirt, piercing his chest. Kye wrenched the dagger back out, kicking the knight away at the same time, and pulled free from his reach.

Hooves beat against cobblestone. Niall was already gone, his horse galloping down the street. Kye made for the remaining steed and leapt onto its back – it snorted, trying to throw him. He didn't let it, ripping away the line hitched around the light-post and turning the horse even as it twisted and bucked. With a firm hand on its neck, it suddenly obeyed his command and galloped instead. Buildings and streets whipped past them.

"My horse!" bellowed the first holy knight, his voice fading as Kye rapidly left them behind. "He stole my *horse!*"

Imperials and their horses— Kye refocused. The horse ran flat out, its breath little more than hard grunting in its chest. He was terrifying the poor beast; he knew that. His metal claws splayed on its neck, points digging gingerly into its hide, made it feel fear born from another realm. Because of this, it followed his command. Kye hated doing it. He liked animals, despite how they didn't at all like him.

Once he felt sure he'd left the knights behind, he slowed the steed and leapt off its back, making immediately for the nearest building. He climbed with the speed and grace of a frightened cat running up a tree. Surveying the streets, he found no pursuers immediately on his trail.

The Templars would surely raise an alarm, however, even without more of their own number in the city. That gave him less time and less freedom to move around Illikon... but at least no one had seen the truth about him. Kye was still merely a criminal to them – a household thief, nothing more, and unworthy of a Templar hunt. Maybe they even believed he was some agent of Faro's. Kye didn't care.

But the knight sensing something evil bothered him. There was no way for a mortal to know the truth about him when he was disguised. No 'sense' lent them such power.

Kye made his way over the rooftop, descending into the next alley and walking the streets. He needed to reach the docks and find Niall. Hopefully, he wasn't too far ahead. And hopefully, he went there at all. Even if he hadn't, Kye would board the *thalamegos* alone. He only hoped Tom Drake would return soon after, so they could formulate a final plan and take him out. But, more than that, Kye hoped the Silent Messengers wouldn't punish him for taking so long assassinating his target...

And that he could recover his sword before it was too late.

PART II – An Innocent Life

Nearing the docks, Kye searched for Niall. He wandered for several minutes, looking over the many large bi- and triremes with their great, colorful sails and prows painted with frightening faces. Rowboats littered the water, tied among the larger boats or toward the ends of the piers. Moonlight cast the sea in a surreal glow, making the water look black and painting the horizon the deepest of ink-blues. Kye found it beautiful.

The docks were quiet, and he felt relief being so alone. Weren't the docks of mortal cities usually busier, though, especially before the dead of night? Maybe the threat of impending war had sent most sailors to taverns, shirking their work and drowning their woes.

"*Psst!*" a voice farther along the docks hissed. Pricking up his ears, Kye found Niall already in a small fishing boat. He held an oar positioned to throw it like a javelin in Kye's direction. "Get over here!"

Kye picked up the pace, joining his partner. The sight of the rowboat, however, made him stop at the edge of the docks and swallow hard. Niall glared up at him from within the low little craft, wearing a face like an angry wet cat despite being perfectly dry. A cat also would have been cute and endearing, which Niall was not.

"What are you waiting for?" Niall snapped.

"I don't like boats," Kye admitted. "Or water."

"Nyx give me strength or else strike you down. I'll be sure to tell Fate not to give us a mission involving boats or water next time. But wait, it didn't *this* time, either. Our mission is to kill a knight back there on land," Niall jabbed a thumb over his shoulder, "not out here retrieving your accursed demonic blade—"

"Will you stop?" Kye hissed, exasperated, and finally lowered himself into the boat. Niall flailed inexpertly trying to keep the ship level once Kye's weight jostled it, but he finally put his hands out and steadied the craft.

"If we sink, I'm blaming you," Niall said flatly.

"I'm sure you are. Good job finding a boat, by the way."

"Do not thank me. I picked one at random and now it's ours. I hope whoever owns it never sees it again and loses all his coin. Perhaps I'll sink it when we get back, to be sure."

"You're really bitter, you know that?"

"Yes. And you're so nice it sickens me. We've discussed this."

Niall shoved a pair of oars toward Kye, who took them silently while Niall untied the boat. Together, they rowed into the open ocean. Now the moonlight was bright enough only to lend credence to imagined dangers, and from this new position, the grey-black water looked more frightening than beautiful. Kye didn't like the idea of anything he might have to swim in, but the ocean bothered him most of all. Memories of water filling his lungs invaded his mind, even if that water had been quite different from any of this mortal world...

Prying his attention from the cresting waves – which he felt threatened their simple boat, though they didn't worry Niall in the least – Kye focused on the distant shape looming like a single mountain peak on the horizon. It was massive, larger than any ship Kye had ever seen, with near-countless tiered rows of oars reaching into the water far below. Atop it towered several structures very much like full buildings, with a single sail larger than Kye fathomed mortals capable of fashioning.

Vast open decks on either side of the structures overlooked the ocean, and even from their distance, Kye made out scores of silhouetted shapes milling around on its surface like dutiful ants. Two heads, two sterns, and four rudders composed the massive vessel that looked almost like two great ships merged together, bearing the dual hulls of a catamaran. Kye marveled at the achievement of having built such a thing, much less operating it in open water primarily using man's own physical strength.

Clouds gathered as they slowly cleared the distance between the Illikon docks and the great ship, the *thalamegos*. Looming shadows steadily blotted out the stars Kye so enjoyed admiring. Within moments, those clouds would also overtake the moon.

"So," Niall said as they rowed, "am I not a good partner, accompanying you on this venture?"

"I'm actually surprised you are, so – yes," Kye replied. "Thank you, Niall."

Hocking up a wad of phlegm, Niall spat over the side of the boat; the expulsion was so sizable it made a noisy splash. "That is what I care of your thanks. I'm only doing this because I need you to kill that knight. Would that I had a far more *professional* partner."

Kye sighed. "Well, thanks anyway." His mind drifted before he added, "I'm still worried about what that Templar said. I've never had even the greatest of holy knights or beings 'sense' anything about me. I don't get it. It's just – not possible."

"He said he sensed evil," Niall replied flatly, "and that clearly means you."

"No one can know what I am. Not like that."

"And you're so confident of this, why? Because you know so much of 'mortals' and our world?"

Kye hesitated. "Because I... *know*. I spent time with someone who *should* have known, long before any mortal could, and..." He shook his head. "It had to be something else. I know it wasn't me."

Niall shrugged. "What mystifies *me* is that a man like Faro, with connections to Kemhet, as rich and powerful as whoever owns that great boat, would live in a barbarian-infested frontier. I thought ships of this size were meant only to traverse rivers, not the sea. The sea might tear one apart. As I said, must have cost a fortune... And here we are risking our hides rowing this little wooden bucket all the way out here."

"We'll be fine," Kye said promptly and entirely for his own sake. "It wouldn't have been tied at the ocean docks if it wasn't an ocean boat, right?"

Niall only chortled through his nose. With that, their conversation ended.

Given that the massive *thalamegos* rested at anchor, they approached it with relative ease. Niall didn't seem too bothered, but Kye initially flinched away from the water lapping the massive ship's hull. Gathering his courage, Kye lifted himself – and sank the claws of his left gauntlet into the thick wood. Niall rose behind him, and Kye outstretched his right hand. Scowling, Niall jumped, catching hold and allowing Kye to pull him up.

They ascended the ship's hull. Kye led, tearing rough handholds with his metal claws. Too often, he felt Niall snatch ahold of his leg and cling for dear life, but Kye never lost his grip. Finally, Kye pulled himself up to an opening devoid of an oar and peered within.

The ship's open wooden belly spread out before him. Toward its center, tiered decks formed a sort of mezzanine like a mighty theatre overlooking the ship's deepest middle. Rows of benches for oarsmen lined the ship's walls, but with the vessel anchored, no one manned them. Still, they were no less busy. Countless men hurried to and fro, hard at work managing the craft. No one noticed Kye peering inside through the lonely and shadowed hole he'd found on the massive ship's far aft.

Voices rang across the decks. Someone shouted about a storm—

Niall grabbed Kye's belt from the side and pulled up with his full bodyweight, nearly tugging Kye's trousers down, the smaller man using Kye's long form like a ladder. Kye threw him a glare. Niall offered no reaction, his dark eyes roaming over the opening. Kye said nothing; he knew, if nothing else, his shoulders wouldn't fit. He'd have to find a proper window.

Niall, however, wormed past him and squeezed through the opening like an octopus. Kye bit back the need to ask if the sweat and grease coating Niall's person helped with such feats. Wearing a fat, triumphant smile, Niall pressed a finger against his lips before pointing upward, ushering Kye to find his own way inside. Kye nodded and resumed climbing.

No windows immediately presented themselves. Kye reached the edge of the first open deck without finding another way inside. Not allowing hesitation, he pulled himself right over, landing neatly on his feet and assuming as casual an air as possible. Still no one noticed; the crew were rushing around with too great a purpose. Kye frowned – and then a sailor suddenly strode right up to him.

The man, a ruddy-skinned Kemheti wearing little other than a white *shendyt* loincloth, glanced him up and down and barked in heavily-accented Imperial Common, "Mercenary! You're quite a wild one. I don't care if you're part of that little cult Faro is getting going, you still have to work. Get below decks and see if they need more men on the oars before this storm hits. Move! Now!"

The man pointed at an open hatch. Unsure if he should puff himself up and refuse, or salute, nod, or whatever else, Kye simply turned on his heel and lowered himself through the hatch in question. Since the Kemheti left, Kye figured he did the right thing. Holding his head high, as if he knew the ship and belonged here, Kye strode among the many harried sailors below decks. Oarsmen now took their places on the benches, but Kye ignored them, scanning for Niall...

His partner weaved among the countless crewmen, finding Kye first. Though Niall stopped, Kye subtly nudged his arm in passing and urged him onward. If they looked unoccupied, it would draw more attention.

"Find anything?" Kye asked.

"Yes," replied Niall. "I found Faro. He strutted about down here like the king of all Emerita. Said he needs blood – an innocent life, or perhaps also a virgin. He's not sure which."

Kye blinked incredulously.

Niall clarified, his voice small, "I think he wishes to summon a demon."

Kye's mouth fell open. Niall looked back at him in silence, his own gaze stony and afraid. He shifted on his feet, and Kye sputtered.

"That— he— *why?* Why would any of you people *want* that?"

"Perhaps he became obsessed after he witnessed one in this gods-forsaken city years ago," replied Niall. "Perhaps it drove him to madness. I know a great deal and pretend to know the rest, but I don't know that. Those who see a demon are never the same, that much I've heard. I only want off this ship. He had your *shamshir* in his belt. Let us kill him, take it, and get out of here."

"Agreed," Kye muttered, leading the way. He looked down the great opening in the middle of the lower decks, giving him a view of the ship's innermost tiers, now filling with hundreds of oarsmen... and his keen eyes lit upon something he hadn't noticed before.

A child.

Bound hand and foot in sturdy ship rope as thick as the child's own meager arms, a little girl was curled into the fetal position near the edge of the railing on an open lower level of the ship. Kye stopped in his tracks, staring. He didn't know mortal age well, but he knew she was only a child. No older than nine years, and perhaps younger than that. She was but a tiny blossom of a mortal in the endless march of time.

Niall wheeled about, throwing his hands out, with frustration in his eyes. But as Niall rejoined him, Kye paid him no heed, his attention on the child. Her long blond hair draped around her like curtains, the way she sat with her knees curled into her chest. Following Kye's eyes, Niall saw her, too. His face betrayed nothing.

"Kye," Niall hissed, "we must leave."

Fury rose in Kye's chest. Hatred, rage – emotions he fought always to suppress. Emotions that led to sin. Evil. Led to him inflicting pain... and even enjoying it.

"Kye—"

"I am *not*," Kye suddenly snarled between his teeth, rounding on his partner, "leaving that little girl to die."

The change in his voice and demeanor cowed Niall, like he'd seen something from another world. Niall shied back, shrinking, his eyes fearful. Even though he knew the kind of killer Niall was, a pang of guilt wracked Kye's heart.

"That's Faro's innocent life – his sacrifice," Kye clarified, calmer now. "That little girl. Faro's going to kill her and feed her soul to a demon." He shook his head. "I can't let that happen, Niall. I've got to save her."

"That little girl be damned!" Niall hissed— and Kye surged forward, grabbing a fistful of Niall's leather as though it was but cloth, curling it in the great talons on his left hand.

He ordered in a voice low and dangerous, "Take that back."

Niall steeled himself and snapped, "I will not!"

"That's a curse, Niall – you take it back, or I'll *show* you what an eaten soul looks like."

Blood drained from Niall's ruddy face, and he set his jaw. Then he blurted, "Fine, I take it back! But children die every day, and sometimes *we* are the ones who kill them! We're not thieves nor saviors nor smiters of demon-worshipers— we are Silent Messengers, or did you forget your own place in this world? Remember who you are, *what* you are – and what the Messengers have done for you!"

The ship lurched.

Kye released Niall, his hand shooting out instead for the nearby deck railing. Niall nearly fell over backward. Their gazes met again, wide-eyed. Finally, they paid attention to the crew hurrying endlessly about them.

"Storm's nearing!" one shouted.

"Anchor's up!" bellowed another.

An even greater bellow came from the Kemheti slave-driver. *"Row!"*

Standing on a deck above, the Kemheti cracked a whip. Though it struck nowhere near him, the sound of its ear-splitting snap ripped down Kye's spine, making him cringe and pinch his eyes shut. He battled a flood of memories that he never wanted to experience again. Every thought hid somewhere he couldn't find it. All his previous conviction and anger fled in an instant. He remembered that he was broken.

"These idiots think they can outrun a storm," Niall declared. "I've heard the storms are getting worse here in the North – the gods of the Achaeans and the gods of Nordlings are threatening war, same as their followers. Nothing like that has happened for hundreds of years. A war in the heavens..."

"Ahriman's blood, please don't say things like that," begged Kye, finally regaining some sense after the whip's crack.

"A storm like this in the coming winter isn't natural. It will tear this ship apart. We must leave. Now."

Kye found his resolve again when his eyes found Faro hurrying to the main deck. Sheathed on his hip was Fang, Kye's own scimitar, forged by Akhoman for Kye alone. Niall was right – they should run, and Kye knew that. But, for once, he spurned the thought. Kye straightened and drew a dagger from the belt across his chest. Such bravery rarely found a home in his heart, and he fought to keep it alive.

"Not until I get back my sword," he said.

"We'll soon leave Illikon *behind!*" Niall hissed, still not raising his voice. "If we get too far to sea, we can't make it back— forget all this idiocy, we must save ourselves! Or we will *all* become sacrifices – *to Poseidon!*"

"Do what you like," answered Kye, brushing past his partner. "I have to see this through."

"What is your plan? You cannot fight him alone, and I'm not going to help."

Kye didn't look back, marching straight toward the stairs Faro had already ascended. "He's only a mortal. I *can* fight him alone."

Behind him, Niall said aloud, "Gods help us."

Kye emerged from the lower decks. Darkness engulfed the ship, leaving the crew nearly blind. Cutting wind bit their skin and eyes. A gale howled across the ship's surface, men frantically rushing over the decks. Kye ignored them. He set his eyes upon Faro, who stood confidently against the coming storm, a hand on the hilt of Kye's scimitar still at rest in his sword-belt.

"Faro Pelagius," Kye said with calm that surprised even him as he crossed the deck with but a dagger in his good hand, the metal claws of his left gauntlet curling like a beast's on display, "you have something that belongs to me."

Stunned, Faro pivoted. He balked at first, seeing Kye towering with his black leather accentuating his powerful build, his assorted armor spikes silhouetted against the semidarkness of the stormy night. But when other crewmen also froze, staring, Faro summoned an arrogant smile and laughed.

"I do?" he mocked, drawing Kye's *shamshir* and revealing the shimming purple gem set in its blade, just above the crosspiece. "As if some ruffian would possess such a beautiful blade – and as if I would stoop to such measures."

Kye narrowed his eyes. "I want it back."

"I have nothing of yours."

Lightning flashed. Shouting continued from every deck. Faro pried his gaze from Kye and looked at the coming storm. Kye didn't spare it a glance, though he saw the churning clouds building in the corner of his vision. His attention remained solely on his target, and he took a step closer.

Thunder rolled across the horizon, echoing over the sea. A shiver ran up Kye's spine at the sound of such fury from the heavens. Did they know he was here? That he had escaped? No – Kye couldn't have been that important. It was only a storm, just the gods taking out frustrations...

Steeling himself, Kye watched Faro regard him again with hesitation on his face. The nobleman wasn't sure if he should fight or run, Kye read that much. Crewmen gathered around them, carrying their own weapons, several Imperials with an assortment of weaponry such as straight-bladed *xiphoi* swords for close-quarters or hooked *falcatas*, while the men from Kemhet wielded crescent blades called *khopeshes* or crescent axes. Many were likely trained fighters. Battling his own fear, Kye spoke again.

"This is your last chance. Give me my sword and you can leave. Don't make me kill you, because I will, and I hate how much I'd enjoy it."

"Enjoy it?" Faro echoed, brandishing Kye's own blade at him. Kye's nostrils flared. "What are you, some mad killer?"

Kye answered, "Pray you never know what I am. Now *give me the sword*."

"Enough of this," said Faro. "Kill him!"

The waiting crewmen charged at once, coming from every angle, four in total. Kye spun on the first, knocking him flat with a punch to the face from his gauntlet. The second, he tripped by sweeping a foot out from under him while ducking low to avoid the blade of another – the third, he stabbed in the leg, directly in an artery that would make him bleed out. The fourth, whose blade swung where Kye's chest had been moments ago, he raked over the chest with his gauntlet-claws while rising, delivering such a heavy blow it sent the man sprawling back.

It happened in a matter of seconds, Kye's every movement flowing like water. Kye wheeled on Faro – only to see him maneuvering behind another group of crewmen. They too ran in, weapons ready. Kye didn't balk, catching one blade in his gauntleted hand and gripping the metal until it snapped to pieces like brittle wood. The man wielding it released the hilt of the broken weapon, fell backward, and scrambled away. Wheeling, Kye threw the remaining shards of broken steel at the face of another attacker.

He fought with precision, grace, and uncharacteristic calm, blocking blows on his gauntlet or dancing away before any struck him. Always he lunged afterward to deliver harsh blows with his fist or claws or a quick stab with his dagger. One by one, the crewmen fell to his onslaught of prowess. Several crawled away or dragged themselves over their fallen fellows in hopes of escape.

But there were too many.

They kept coming. This ship held thousands, and even with so many oarsmen occupied below-decks, Kye couldn't stand alone. Despite the storm drawing ever nearer, several crewmen prioritized Kye's threat thanks to the shouting and gesturing of Faro, who ordered them away from their posts to fight Kye instead. Not all obeyed him, but enough did. Blades sang past Kye's chest, his head, one cut him across the arm— they would overwhelm him. No matter how hard he fought, they didn't fear him. Not yet. Right now, he appeared as but an ordinary man... something he was not.

He didn't want to do it. But, at last, Kye released his hold over his human disguise – and revealed his true form.

Wings emerged from his back, huge and terrifying, not unlike the wings of a dragon but with a dark leathern hide in place of scales. Spreading them wide, Kye buffeted the air around him with enough force that his attackers stumbled back.

He spun in place, his evil power on full display. An equally as dark and leathery tail, tipped in a spearhead, extended from his spine; he grew long fangs; vicious scars few could even survive appeared across his skin, some carven patterns of unspeakable tongues and many intertwined with tapering tattoos of black and purple; and his ears became sharply pointed.

Four horns grew on his head, a shorter pair on his forehead and a much longer pair sweeping back atop his skull. Where once he had raven black locks, his hair became a strange hue at once deep and bright, shimmering dark but also vivid purple unnaturally in the light. His sky-blue irises turned a terrible bright violet, full of black magic...

Silence fell for but a moment. The ship and everyone on it stilled. Terror filled the air. Even the storm around them seemed to fall quiet at the revelation.

Until someone screamed, *"Demon!"*

Once-bold fighters screamed that all should run and begged for mercy from the gods. Crewmen fell over one another, escape now their only goal. They fled before him like frightened children, all bravery and loyalty spent at the sight of a man-shaped creature born of such darkness. What stood before them now, in their mortal eyes, was no warrior – it was nothing one could fight and kill. It was not even human. It was an aberration of utmost evil, created of their own misdeeds and sent to inflict horror upon the world. It would punish their very souls, reveling in their mortal sin. Those who witnessed it saw only reflections of every wrongfully fulfilled temptation, every ill – and their own awaiting, eternal doom.

Right now, Kye wouldn't try convincing them otherwise. None here had hearts true enough to stand against a thing like him, as would have the holy knight he'd fled from before. He'd make full use of the advantage.

Only Faro remained entirely still, staring, though certainly not from a good heart. Horror twisted his face, but so did fascination – even admiration. He was mystified. Kye's bright gaze locked with the nobleman's, and of all things to witness, he saw envy.

Faro gaped. Kye heard his horrified voice utter over the storm, "What... *what* are *you?*"

Lifting his horned head, Kye answered, "I am something that wears the sins of mortals in my flesh... and I will make you pay for yours."

The storm struck.

As though in retribution for Kye's unwelcome presence in the mortal world, wind tore across the deck with newfound fury. Wood splintered. Bolts of lightning flicked overhead, casting everything in flashes of blinding white. Rain hammered the ship like a million tiny arrows, whipping and roaring, a vortex twisting in every direction. Being trapped in such a gale was one of Kye's greatest fears, yet he stood against it because he had no choice. Spreading his feet and anchoring himself against the wind, Kye – his eyes purple beacons piercing the darkness and wind and rain – held himself low and watched as Faro steadied himself using a nearby railing.

"Give me back my blade, mortal!" Kye roared. "Or so help me, I'll take your soul before your gods can judge it!"

"I don't fear you, demon!" Faro shouted back fruitlessly, voice shattered from fear.

Three brave crewmen rushed Kye from the side, hoping he hadn't seen them – and hoping in vain. Kye lifted his gauntleted hand. Violet glow covered his eyes. Purple-white tendrils of lightning licked from under his sharp brow, a faint red glow like molten lava deep in his skin pulsed beneath the metal gauntlet – and a jolt of power shot forth not from the storm, but from the palm of Kye's hand.

The violet lightning passed through all three men who charged him, stopping them in their tracks. They went rigid, screaming – and then collapsed on the deck, writhing in agony, too weak to move.

The same instant, Kye's visage changed. His horns grew longer still, his wings larger, and his eyes did not reassume a more human appearance. No one else dared approach him then – no one, save Faro.

Whether arrogance or madness lent him such courage, Faro rushed and struck with Kye's blade. Kye reflexively lifted his left hand to catch the blow – only for agony to pass through his arm. The scimitar cut the thick metal gauntlet like his own flesh. Hissing in pain, Kye pulled away and leapt back, shaking out his hand.

"Cannot face your own otherworldly steel, demon?" taunted Faro, gaining confidence.

"Are you *crazy?*" Kye shouted over the storm, his tone familiar again rather than that of a monster. "Your ship is sinking and you're still fighting me over a sword!? Just give it to me before we *all* die!"

"Never! I will use it to summon another – or else I will use it to enslave *you* and have *your* power!"

The ship lurched. Kye stumbled, nearly losing his footing. He barely heard himself think over the wind and rain. One of the many doors below decks flew open and a sailor barged out.

"She's taking on water!" he shouted, making for the vessel's port side. "Abandon ship! Stay together!"

His voice was nearly lost in the cacophony of wind and screaming and prayers to Poseidon and Set. "Demon!" "Lower the boats!" "It has cursed us!" "Set, deliver us from these foreign waters!"

Oarsmen, hundreds or even thousands of them, appeared from the lower decks. They clambered up hatches and ran up stairs, ascending ladders with such haste that some thoughtlessly trampled others. A surge of humanity made for the lifeboats, but Kye remained focused on his target.

He sliced Faro with his dagger. With the small blade's short reach, even with his long arms, he couldn't get in a stab without risking himself against Faro's defenses. Faro moved back, the blow minor, and swept the scimitar around. It cut Kye's bare right arm, trailing blood, but Kye showed no weakness. They resumed circling each other even as the ship's crew continued their disorganized escape.

Faro attacked again. Kye didn't dodge, bringing up his only weapon and snatching the *shamshir* near the hilt, their blades grinding together at the crosspieces. Kye knew he couldn't hold it for long. He felt lucky the dagger didn't simply break under the unnatural might of the sword.

"You want a demon's power – but didn't one of your land's own knights prove that Men don't need it?" Kye stayed his ground, his strength so considerable against Faro's that he held back the scimitar even with such a small blade. "What about the Demon Slayer? What about Tom Drake?"

"To hell with Tom Drake!" Faro shouted back. "It's *his* fault my nephew died to that demon! If it wasn't for him, Radek would still be alive... Now only a demon can bring him back! *That* is why I need your power!"

"Bring him back!? Demons can't do that— he'd be a husk! Your nephew is gone – he's with your gods and ancestors!"

"You will aid me or return to your abyss!" Faro shrieked.

They separated again, pulling their blades apart. Faro nearly pried the dagger from Kye's grip, but he slid it free, dancing back a pace or two. Faro's free hand shot to his belt, and from it he pulled a small bottle. He threw it at Kye – and struck true.

The glass shattered on Kye's broad chest. Colorless liquid splashed across his form, touching some bare skin of his neck and arms. It looked and felt like water, but it burned like boiling pitch. Kye yelled in pain, panicking, trying to swipe the liquid off him with his left hand. It already singed his flesh, and still its touch lingered, the agony biting deeper than any acid.

Holy water. Kye's insides twisted, recoiling at the thought. Thankfully, only a small amount had touched his skin...

"You truly *are* evil, then, man-demon!" Faro cried. "How did you even come to this world? Why do you, a twisted thing of shadow, accuse *me* of sin when you yourself are born of it?"

Kye didn't answer. Any protests would emerge weak, and Faro didn't deserve his words any more than he deserved his mercy. But fear wound its way into him along with hatred – and the knowledge that Faro was right. Kye was born of evil, though not entirely. Unlike true demons, which were manifestations of sin spawned from a pit, Kye was born of a human parent, who had gifted him with a soul. That offered him a choice between good and evil, same as Faro's own soul did.

But Faro chose evil, even without a demonic taint in his blood crying out for it constantly. That thought drove away Kye's horror at the touch of holy water and let his fury return.

Kye gnashed his teeth, his fangs as long as a vampire's. In desperate rage, he threw out his hand – and again a bolt of purple lightning shot from it. But rather than hitting Faro, who leapt aside in an ungraceful but effective dodge, Kye's wild power struck the ship instead.

Wood, marble, and metal warped, twisting and sundering, as the bolt of unholy lightning split across the upper deck of the ship. The structures in the center of the vessel cracked, a gaping hole blown through their middle. Several deck-boards flew to pieces from the unnatural power twisting the air, splinters flying, singed and smoldering red. But Kye did not relent. He lost himself.

Rushing in once more, Kye lunged for Faro's middle, no longer caring about injury. The nobleman stepped aside, slashing Kye across the chest as he did – but he stepped directly into Kye's waiting, outstretched hand. His left hand. Claws gripped Faro's throat. Ignoring his own scimitar that still pushed hard into his skin through the jerkin he wore, Kye drove forward and lifted Faro off his feet. The scimitar lifted with him, leaving blood on Kye's rent armor. Try though he did to strike Kye with the weapon again, Faro's efforts became weak.

"Give me," Kye snarled, "my *sword*."

"T-take it!" Faro choked, legs kicking. His boots hit Kye wherever they could reach. Kye didn't react, looking Faro in the eye. The blows meant nothing.

Kye hauled Faro ever higher – and slammed him back-first into the deck. Faro wheezed, stunned, and released the *shamshir*. Kye scooped up the blade in his right hand, where it belonged. Faro twisted pathetically beneath him, gripping Kye's spiked left forearm, the sharp metal piercing Faro's skin. His legs flailed uselessly, his entire body writhing. He gagged and sputtered. Any decent person suffering so would've stirred sympathy in Kye's soul, yet this time, he felt none.

"I should hurt you," said Kye, his shadowed, glowing pits of eyes locked with Faro's. "I should show you pain for what you wanted to do to that little girl."

Confusion and surprise filled Faro's wide, terrified stare. Kye tightened his grip on Faro's throat, ensuring he didn't speak. His voice would not be heard again.

"Yes," he finished, "I saw her. I know you wanted to sacrifice her to a demon. And there's something in me that'd love to torture you for that, maybe even take your soul for myself – but if I *did* do that, I'd become closer to the monster you say I am. Even though you don't deserve it, I'll show you mercy."

For a moment, Faro's struggling went still. He waited despite being denied air, bloodshot eyes bulging from his reddened face. He must have thought Kye's mercy meant letting him go. How wrong he was.

Kye tightened his grip. Faro squirmed one last time, tongue protruding as he fought uselessly for air – just before Kye felt the nobleman's windpipe collapse. Faro went still.

Kye ripped the sword-belt from Faro's corpse, returning it to his own hip and sheathing his blade. He arose – only to cringe at another crack of thunder that rattled his bones. He ducked low in fear. Lightning flashed on all sides, stinging his eyes, licking through the clouds and threatening every moment to strike the ship. Kye tucked his great wings close. He hated storms – such violent, unchained displays of the gods' power. They were terrifying, and this was the worst he'd ever seen.

Pressure built in his chest. The rain slashed harder than ever and struck his body like whip-lashes. With the battle over and his blood silenced for now, the sting of his many wounds came on suddenly and reminded him how much he hated pain.

Another crack split the air – but not from the heavens. It came from the ship. Everything lurched, throwing Kye forward on his face. He landed in a heap, scrambling and setting his claws into the wood before he slid toward the edge of the deck, as the world tilted against a massive wave. A short cry of terror escaped his throat. Crates and barrels and even a few still-fleeing crewmen slid and tumbled before they crashed into the raging sea. The wave hurtled the ship along with it—wind rushed past him, free and open, as if the entire craft was airborne – before it fully met with the ocean once more.

The massive *thalamegos* righted itself again, sickeningly. Kye's stomach remained somewhere at the bottom of the last cresting surge. He wanted to be sick. His head throbbed with the racing of his heart, his ears popping at him, the very air crushing inward around his skull. Almost no crewmen remained. Kye pulled himself back to his feet and assessed the near-empty deck. Creaking and splintering as it was, he knew the ship would give any moment.

Running to a far side, Kye scanned the many dinghies fighting perilously against the wild sea. The sailors rowed madly in hope of escape before the worst struck...

Among them, Kye recognized the dark shape of Niall. He occupied the same boat he and Kye had used to reach the *thalamegos* in the first place, only now several other men had joined him, helping row. Waves tossed the lifeboats like corks. Several overturned even as he watched. Men spilled into the unforgiving ocean, many never resurfacing. In the face of such a grisly death, alliances no longer mattered. The mortals wished only to escape with their lives – and so did Kye.

He hesitated. This wasn't yet the heart of the storm. Not even a ship as great as this would survive against the fury awaiting in the next few precious moments. Kye still had a chance. He could escape with his life, before the worst of the storm hit... or he could save that little girl doubtlessly still bound beneath the decks.

Bile burned in his throat. Weakness and trembling settled in his limbs. Terror gripped his soul. If he went to save the child, he might not make it. They would both die, caught on the sinking ship. Trapped. Suffocating in total darkness, struggling themselves to exhaustion. They would drown, unable to escape. Kye's incredible power would be useless against the rage of the sea and the layers of ship that would collapse upon them. Their deaths would be one of the worst imaginable.

On a ship like this, in a storm like this, going back for the child spelled certain doom. After much suffering and fear, Kye would finally die and then awaken in the Underworld. His years of work, unknown ages of struggle, misery, and horror would be undone. Everything would be as it once was, and the child too would be dead.

But, if he did nothing, she was dead anyway – and she would face that fate alone.

"Blood and shadow," Kye cursed aloud. He turned his back on the open air, the sea, and his fleeing partner. He ran straight for the hatch leading below decks.

He had to save that little girl.

Kye stormed down the hatch, landing hard on his heavy feet with no attempted grace. He scanned the ship interior – but pitch black engulfed everything. No candles or lanterns lit the area anymore, save for one or two lamps still somehow burning, hanging precariously on hooks, their existence as doomed as Kye felt. Water had reached the others and extinguished them, if they hadn't been taken by crewmen during the evacuation.

Darkness pervaded every lower deck, but Kye's eyes rapidly adjusted. Shadow in the Underworld and Nidavellir, realms far beneath Midgard, was so much deeper than this simple mortal darkness that he still saw almost perfectly – and he saw little more than destruction. He smelled brine so strongly it was nearly stifling in the enclosed space. Running to the first railing of the many tiers, Kye looked straight down, where the child had been before—

She was still there. Kye saw her long, pale hair as she squirmed and struggled. The bonds around her wrists and ankles were firmly anchored to something, though Kye didn't know what. Two tiers down, water cascaded into the vessel, filling it rapidly. He didn't have much time.

Kye vaulted over the railing, spreading his wings enough to slow his fall and glide for the edge of the ship's third tier, where the girl was tied. Reaching it, he hoisted himself up, landing much quieter this time. The girl didn't look at him, probably not even hearing nor seeing him, as hopelessly focused as she was on her bonds. Rushing water and his own racing heart filled his ears, but Kye closed his eyes.

Assuming his human disguise in times of stress was something he'd practiced extensively. Even under the threat of death, he could maintain a human appearance. Now, especially having called upon his demonic power and given in to his inner darkness even as much as he had, it was very difficult. But he had to. He *had* to – the little girl couldn't see him like this.

The Silent Messengers had killed witnesses for him in the past, protected his secret for their own sake more than his. He wouldn't let that happen to this child. His right hand found the back of his neck, and he gripped it hard, pinching his eyes shut tighter and making himself focus.

Through sheer force of will, he hid his sundry demonic features again. He approached the child, kneeling – and big blue eyes looked up at him, reddened and sopping with tears. She sobbed, her crying jolting her entire body. Kye wasn't sure the child even saw him well at all, it was so dark, but he wouldn't risk anything.

Holding up his empty palms, despite the great clawed gauntlet on his left hand, he said, "I won't hurt you. Let me help."

The child only stared, eyes wide as dinner plates. Kye reached out with his right hand, using his human fingers to pull the rope gag from the little girl's mouth. She sputtered but didn't speak, twisting in her bonds. Her efforts to move away proved useless, the ropes around her tied to a stake firmly implanted in the wood underfoot. But with a careful grip and twist of Kye's claws, the ropes came free. He pulled them off her while she squirmed – and, the instant she was capable, she scrambled away from him and curled up against a far portion of the railing.

"Wait!" Kye said, showing his palms again. "The ship's falling apart – you have to trust me!"

She stared.

He added carefully, "I'm scared too. But I'm here to help."

She stared.

Kye reached for his belt, pulling free the striped cat toy he'd found in Faro's home. The soft little thing squished in his hand. He held it out to her.

"This is yours, isn't it?" he said. "Take it— take it and let me get you outta here. I *promise* I won't hurt you."

The little girl hesitated. The ship creaked and rocked. Groaning filled his ears, the vessel voicing its coming demise. Kye's hand found the railing again, steadying himself where he knelt. Thunder rolled and crashed as continuously as the sea, echoing in the confined space, and water still rushed in far below...

"Please," Kye said again, as gently as his shaking voice could muster. He grasped hard at his will that he might maintain a human guise. "C'mon— we have to get out of here and we need to be fast."

Suddenly, the child scrambled forward and snatched the toy from his hand. She clutched it against her chest. Kye wrapped his right arm around her, pulling her close, but she was so small and slight that he feared he'd break her if he held on too hard.

"It'll be okay," Kye said, with no idea what to say at all. "Hold it tight. And hold on to *me*. Whatever happens, don't let go... and don't look."

He arose with the little girl clutching the bandoleer across his chest. She stuffed the little plush animal back into his belt, holding onto him with both hands and burying her face.

Kye wheeled. He made for the exit again. It was just ahead: a doorway leading to the stairs connecting the next few decks, including the top one. Not far to run...

The distance widened. Shifted. The world changed, the floor rising under his feet. Kye lost his footing. The entire ship tipped backward, making Kye's head spin, disorienting him— he felt he left every one of his organs behind as the world pitched up on its back, the ship's nose pointing toward the heavens. Kye yelled as he fell, backward, toward the far side of the now upended, massive vessel. It would be a long fall.

The railing – under him – he saw it, sideways, no longer a railing now but a ledge as the floor turned to a sheer wooden face before him, like the wall of a building. Without his wings, all he could do was grab for it. He needed his wings...

The little girl slipped, fell free, her grip failing. Kye panicked. Straw-gold hair all but glowed against the darkness. She was but a small shape falling past him, hurtling toward oblivion—

His disguise fell away at once. He spread his wings for balance, his wing-claws found the railing – and his long, spaded tail reached for the child before she plummeted beyond. It coiled around her middle with precision, catching her, holding on too tight for her to slip free. Reflexively, she held on to the thing that saved her. Kye felt her recoil in horror the instant her fingers touched it. Her high scream pierced the roar of the storm and sea. Kye's heart turned inside out, squeezing up into his throat.

With his left hand, he got a firmer hold of the railing above. He hung from it, his long form dangling in the open center of the vessel. He lifted the little girl with his tail until he took hold of her with his right hand instead. Her huge blue eyes looked up at him, at his face – and he pinched his eyes shut, turning his face away. Even in the darkness, she would see his purple eyes.

"Don't look— *please* don't look," he panted, hoisting her back up to his chest. She grabbed hold. Deftly, he undid the buckle of his bandoleer and slid it over her, fastening it with the child held firmly against him beneath the belt.

The ship pitched again. This time, Kye was ready for it.

As it fell, Kye went with it. He pulled himself upward and then sideways as the ship's prow once again tilted level with the sea. His boots kicked off the railing, flipping him midair – and he spread his wings, catching himself.

Which way was up now? Which way was down? Kye hardly knew. He didn't care. He only wanted to escape. High overhead, lightning flashed through a great hole in a reaching building atop the *thalamagos*'s back. Disoriented but at least seeing the sky, Kye buffeted his wings.

Water poured around him. It rushed from the decks overhead. Debris collapsed everywhere, a piece of wood striking his shoulder so hard he cried out. Salt-water filled his mouth, his nostrils. He had no idea if he was in the air, in the water, where he was, if he could even still breathe—

A massive, thundering boom shook him to his core, filling his ears and echoing through his innards. The ship was on its belly again. Kye flailed, scrambled, hands searching for any hold. Everything was water – no wood, no surface. He flexed his wings, kicked, surging upward, toward air.

He broke the surface, gasping, blinking his burning eyes and quickly swimming for the railing of the ship's uppermost lower deck. He pulled himself up, feet at last finding a surface again, and coughed a bucket of water from his lungs. Still the little girl clung to his chest, held fast by the belt, also sputtering seawater.

More deafening than ever, creaking shook the floorboards, nearly knocking Kye off-balance. He found his footing – and turned barely in time to witness the ship break in half.

It snapped, louder than the thundering of a demon lord's fury. The two halves shuddered – then the ship split down the middle. Flashing lightning poured inside, rain and wind ripping into the opening, rushing air deafeningly filling the space. The latter half of the ship collapsed into the surging ocean, now a wild and unknowable mass of raging water.

He saw the aft of the ship's corpse – huge splintered boards, mighty sail, shattered buildings, and all – fall away from the first half. Its bulk lifted with the next wave, but a toy to the gods, a symbol of mankind's foolish pride reduced to nothing. Structures from atop the *thalamegos* fell to pieces and scattered in the ocean, other pieces thrown away and farther afield by the sheer roaring wind. Between the thunder and the cracking sunder of the wood and ship's entire structure, the air endlessly reverberated with pounding destruction.

Kye backed up, spun, and once more made for the hatch. He scrambled with all haste, claws and fingernails scraping wood. His mind screamed at him. His heart raced. He turned in a circle, wondering how he'd survive, and saw nothing. This was it. He was about to die.

Ahead. The ship's prow, long nose pitching upward again. Up toward the open sky – and the storm. But there was no other choice.

Kye ran.

Boots eating the deck, long legs charging as fast as they could carry him, Kye focused only on the prow of the once proud *thalamegos*. Lightning lit the world. The prow towered like a spire out into nothing, a dark silhouette, his only hope against the furious ocean that surged ever closer. He heard it, felt it, smelled it, tasted it – the water was coming, the broken ship was sinking fast...

He tore up the ship's prow, running, leaping – he made for the farthest point – then he kicked off. Fully spreading his vast wings, he jumped into open air. Wind caught and filled the membrane of those mighty demonic limbs. It lifted him upward, away from the water – and then pitched him sideways.

Kye fought to compensate. The wild gale fought back, tossing him in every direction. Surging all his might into his chest and back, he pushed against it, buffeting his wings again. If he touched the water, he was dead. It would take hold and not let go. All that mattered was staying in the air.

Thunder ripped into his skull. Lightning blinded him. He felt the impossible amount of heat off a bolt and wondered how he wasn't dead. He was a good flier, one of the few things at which he truly prided himself, but never had he been so insane as to fly in a storm such as this one.

He wrapped his right arm around his chest. The little girl was still there, snug between the belt and his body, holding on for dear life. Kye's arm stayed around her while his wings fought the wind. He felt deaf and blind, ears ringing, heart pounding...

Why the gods of Men did not strike him down, Kye didn't know. Perhaps they were trying. Perhaps only the presence of a child's innocence kept him alive. But alive he was, and he even saw a tiny light far in the distance, through the wind and rain. A lantern. A boat. Survivors.

Kye twisted in the air. Flying in such a storm was chaos and agony. It took every ounce of his strength to control his wings, every buffet of them an impossible effort that squeezed burning pain deep into his already exhausted muscles and injured body. He went up, then down, then sideways, assaulted always by the endless smattering of rain and pellets of ice. Thunder seemed caught in his very insides, lightning burned his eyes—

And then, it began to fade.

Kye righted himself, holding steady. He looked over his shoulder and wing at the storm. Such a great and terrible thing, a black mass against the already black night, lit so frequently by shocks of lightning that one might imagine it unnatural. Booming thunder still rolled over the horizon as he left the wind and rain behind. For all its power, however, the storm was not as large as he thought... and, from here, it was strangely beautiful.

Relief filled his veins, but exhaustion came with it. Pain held his weary body together, and only now did he realize his chest was dark in his own blood. Some also trickled down his arm, mixing with the brine there. He hadn't realized during the struggle for survival just how badly the salt water made his wounds burn.

Far below, an assembly of dinghies stretched toward the distant view of Illikon. None would welcome a monster such as him, save one... He picked it out quickly – a larger rowboat. Beneath them, Niall pushed a corpse into the water. Alone in his reclaimed dinghy, he must've killed every other man with him and tossed them into the sea once they were relatively safe from the storm.

Calmer winds filled his wings, helping Kye guide himself for Niall's craft. Niall didn't look up, focused on his one-man rowing act all the way back to Illikon – and Kye landed suddenly in a heap, once again nearly flipping the boat.

Niall swore curses most vile, throwing his limbs this way and that in hopes of keeping their small vessel aright. Kye barely noticed, collapsing with what little room he had, much of his huge wings draping into the ocean. Niall gaped. Kye finally opened his eyes and regarded him, blinking slowly.

Kye said nothing, breathing hard, finally letting his body relax. The little girl didn't budge. Niall only kept staring, his eyes threatening to pop out of his head.

After a moment longer, Kye gathered what strength remained and sat upright. Right hand still gently pressing the child's head against him so she wouldn't open her eyes, he refocused. Every demonic feature once more reverted, lessening, disappearing – and Niall recoiled in horror.

Kye frowned. "It's not even gross," he said, voice coming out weak. Maybe he'd screamed more than he'd realized.

"It is disgusting. It's unholy and vile and I never want to witness that, or *it*, again—"

Kye glared at him. Niall shut up – and finally looked at the mess of blond hair and slight form tucked against Kye's body. His lips twitched.

"I am not sure whether to be impressed or disgusted with your skillful waste of our time and meaningless heroics," he said flatly. "And we're lucky you didn't upend this boat. Again."

"I didn't *actually* upend it before," Kye retorted. He unclasped the belt from around his chest, sliding it away from the child and fixing his bandoleer back again. Leaning low and then lower still, and even lower than that, he looked the little girl in the face. She kept her eyes pinched shut so tightly Kye wondered if it hurt.

"It's okay," he said softly. He found the little animal she'd stuffed in his waist-belt, though it was now soaked, and set it in the boat nearby. "You're okay. And so is your... little... um, thing. It's really wet now, though."

"The child likely talks with more wits than you," remarked Niall.

Kye ignored him. With his good hand, he brushed a human finger over the little girl's cheek, wiping away some of his blood. He bit his lip. He'd have to make sure she didn't have any blood on her before they reached Illikon...

At length, she cracked one eye open, then the other. She blinked. Kye still felt he knew little of mortals and what emotions or traumas plagued them, yet he knew she wasn't right. 'In shock,' he thought Men called it. He had no idea what to do.

Suddenly, her tiny voice asked: "Did the gods send you?"

Kye stared. His face went blank, and his stomach fell through the bottom of the boat. Unable to find his voice, his mouth opened, but nothing came out. A thousand thoughts and fears raced through his mind.

"We... we flew," she continued, so quietly even Kye's sharp ears nearly strained to hear her. "We were *flying*... and there was a snake... or something. I think there's a god with a pet snake..."

Niall laughed a single guffaw so loudly it rattled the phlegm in his throat. Kye remained too stunned for words, his gaze falling to the bottom of the vessel. He'd lied about many things in his life, but he dared not lie about this.

"Good that she does not remember what she saw," remarked Niall, "or at least cannot make sense of it. Who can blame her? *I* scarcely can, and she's but a peasant child. Likely she knows nothing of..."

"Just— be quiet," Kye snapped, though his voice broke oddly. Niall chuckled again, apparently well recovered from his own shock.

"Fine, but let's at least distribute what we can of this weight. We cannot separate *your* lanky bulk, so put that child over here with me."

The little girl recoiled. She slid closer to Kye and clung around his middle. Kye didn't stop her, giving Niall a harsh look from under the shadow of his sharp brow.

"No," Kye replied. "You wouldn't even help me save her."

No oars remained save the two Niall had, any extras doubtlessly lost when Niall murdered the sailors, so Kye let Niall row. He feared for the little girl, wishing desperately she would speak again. Resting his right hand over the child's back, he heaved a sigh and let his eyes fall shut. With half his mind still focused on maintaining his disguise, rest was impossible, but at least he loosened up a little.

Niall's voice near instantly stirred Kye from his imperfect peace. "I cannot believe this happened over your pride," he remarked.

Kye said nothing.

"Or whatever it is you'd call it. A stolen blade. And then you also go out of your way to save useless children, despite being... what you are. I wish the Master had given me a different partner and saddled someone else with your unfortunate and confused existence."

"You mentioned all that," Kye replied acidly.

The water finally calmed, and so too did the churning in Kye's stomach. After a moment longer of Niall rowing, Kye saw Illikon's docks in the distance. The ocean glittered in the light of the moon and stars, the storm now far out at sea. Here, everything felt so peaceful. Though Kye still hadn't recovered from all that happened, at least he breathed easier. Now all he needed was firm ground beneath his boots...

Shifting in his seat, he regarded the little girl again. She peered back at him, eyes focusing this time.

"Do you know where your parents are?" Kye asked.

She nodded. Kye waited, but she said nothing for several moments longer.

Finally, she answered slowly, "My dad is gone." She sounded half dazed, but at least she spoke. "He saved us from the monster."

Kye screwed up his brow in confusion but dared not ask.

"And... my brother's gone too... and... now my mom and I live in the big city where people protect us."

Niall laughed again, even louder this time. "Good job they did, eh?"

"Will you shut up, Niall?" Kye snapped. This time, Niall fell quiet in an instant.

The child seemed unaffected. She scooted onto one of Kye's legs, hugging her knees to her chest and tightening into a nearly perfect ball.

"We used to live on the farm," she said, her voice distant. "I miss the farm."

The Northwoman... Kye remembered suddenly, when he and Niall were in the city, they'd passed by a woman making such a fuss that Kye had wandered closer. The woman had been a Nordling with long, blond hair. Kye glanced down at the little girl's own hair.

"I think I might've seen your mom..."

The little girl didn't respond. She only rocked slightly on his leg.

Kye peered at her again. "My name's Kye," he added gently.

"I thought," sniped Niall, "your name is currently Seth."

"Nope, it's Kye."

The child's big blue eyes met his again before she answered, "My name's Sophie."

Kye managed a small smile. "Okay, Sophie. I'm gonna take you home."

At long last, they reached Illikon. Kye grabbed the nearest dock with his claws, hauling them closer and tying the boat off. The little girl, Sophie, watched him all the while in captivated wonderment, like she observed some great, strange animal. She once again clutched her little soft cat-shaped toy, even though it was still wet. Niall sneered and tossed the oars into the bottom of the rowboat before climbing out.

Kye picked up Sophie. She clung to him like a bug while he hauled himself out of the boat. He nearly flipped it over before jumping up onto the docks, thinking about how much he hated the ocean. Niall watched critically, arms crossed. The thick brows like dead caterpillars on his face formed a perfect, unimpressed line over his eyes.

"I do not believe this," he said flatly.

"You mentioned *that* already too," replied Kye, gently putting Sophie back on her feet. She wobbled for a moment, having not actually stood in a while, much less on firm ground instead of a wallowing ship. "I'm taking her to her mother."

"Fine. I don't care."

Sophie shuffled nearer to Kye and whispered loudly, "He's ugly."

Kye laughed. Niall sneered in disgust at the sight of his handsome smile, as if joy itself wronged him.

"Yes, you mannerless little girl," said Niall with pride, "I am ugly. That's why I work in the shadows. My actions are even uglier. Have you not seen night-creatures, like the beetles? I am one of them."

"Night bugs also bang headfirst into lanterns..." Kye commented.

"I'm leaving. Take your worthless prize and return it, 'Seth,' or else ransom her and make her useful. Perhaps you can get enough coin to buy polish for your precious scimitar. Either way, we have work to do. Find me at the inn."

Niall pivoted and marched off, but before he left, he stopped at a nearby crate and dug something out. He tucked it under his arm, then disappeared. Kye shook his head. Meanwhile, Sophie craned her neck looking up at him.

"Why's he so grouchy?" she asked, suddenly a child again instead of a traumatized little shape. It was an honest question, not a smart remark.

"Because he's a horrible person," replied Kye. "There's really no helping some people. They just have a lot of bad in them, and they don't fight it. Anyway," he held out his human hand, covered only by a fingerless leather glove, "wanna find your mom?"

Sophie slid her hand into his fingers. They left the docks, though Kye felt increasingly wary with each step into Illikon. Quiet reigned over the lamplit streets, save for the sound of the nearby ocean. Few people stirred, with only a couple figures and groups walking the lanes. A pair of city watchmen shot a confused look at the heavily armed, black-leather and spiked-armored figure walking with a child – an unusual sight, to be sure. Kye kept his gaze forward, and

Sophie continued ambling along innocently, hurrying to keep pace with Kye's long strides and never releasing his hand. The watchmen didn't bother them.

Eventually, Sophie took the lead, tugging him along in excitement. She knew where home was. Meanwhile, Kye's mind wandered. Faro, he thought again, had been right. Kye *was* born of evil. The difference was, he fought it, locked in constant battle against his true nature. The little girl beside him reminded him of that. Seeing her eyes bright and wondering again, the fear and trauma already buried for the time being, gave his soul wings... and not ones with wretched black claws. It brought him some small measure of peace, brief as it would be.

Saving Sophie, he thought, was just another little victory in the battle for his own soul – a victory that could easily be overcome, should he lose himself to the dark pulls inside him again. It was a never-ending war. One small action only briefly chased away his inescapable demonic corruption, the same power he'd called forth on the ship.

Had he saved her for selfish reasons? He told himself he hadn't. It hadn't felt like it at the time. Now, he almost wondered, but he dismissed the fear. No matter what, she was alright, and that was all that mattered. Perhaps the stories were true, the gods really did protect children and save their minds from horrors unknowable to the innocence of their age. Kye at least thanked Ahriman, the only deity he knew wouldn't smite him, for that— even knowing Ahriman certainly had the opposite of any hand in it.

They approached a small home, the same one Kye recalled. Sophie ran up in such a hurry that Kye let her hand slide free of his, staying his ground.

She knocked on the door without stopping. "Momma! Momma, I'm home!"

Movement erupted from within. The robust Nordling woman from before threw open the door and scooped her daughter into her arms at once. "Sophie!" she cried. "Oh, my little girl!"

Kye kept his distance. He smiled but didn't say a word, carefully moving a few paces away. With any luck, he might escape unnoticed – but Sophie caught him.

"Kye!" she called, squirming free of her mother's arms and running after him fearlessly. She reached for his nearest hand – but retracted the motion, as she nearly touched his spiked gauntlet. She tugged on his leg instead. "Wait, don't go!"

Sophie's mother watched, confused. Kye looked slightly mortified. Being thanked was the last thing he wanted, though he couldn't fully explain why. He froze like a thief caught red-handed.

"Momma, he saved me," Sophie explained, pointing up at Kye. "I dunno how, but he did. There was a ship and a storm and all these smelly sailors, and..."

The Northwoman approached. Sophie fell quiet. The mother looked deeply into Kye's eyes like she knew too much. Kye swallowed, his right hand wandering up and rubbing the back of his neck.

Throwing out her arms, she pulled Kye into a hug, pressing him against her considerable bosom. Kye went rigid in surprise.

"You saved my daughter, sir," said the woman, ending the hug to lock eyes with him again. "You saved the only child I have left. I fear I can never repay you."

"I don't need payment," Kye replied. "I really don't. Bringing her home was enough."

Tears rose in the woman's already weeping eyes. "May all the gods bless you, sir. You've done a better kindness to me than I have ever received. I don't know what I could do for you, but should you ever need anything – anything at all, even but a roof over your head and a hot meal – I will see it done. Or if you need those wounds tended, I'll do that to the best of my ability."

Kye's insides tied in a knot at the idea of such a blessing, of the gods taking notice of him, but he forced a small smile regardless. "I appreciate that. But I... I'd better go."

Sophie clung to his leg again. "Why can't you stay?" she said. "Just a little while?"

Kye shook his head. "I'm sorry, but – I can't."

"Will I ever see you again?" she blurted.

He hesitated. Bit his lip. He glanced at Sophie's mother, who looked curious for the same answer – but she nodded understandingly.

"Maybe," said Kye. "Maybe— someday."

"I really hope so."

"Sophie, come," said her mother, and Sophie returned to her. The woman scooped her up in another hug but kept her eyes on Kye. "My name is Helga," she said. "May I at least know yours?"

"Kye," he answered.

Concern, though subtle and brief, passed over the woman's face. "Never heard such a name before, not even in talk of men from Kemhet and those far-southern lands."

Against all reason, Kye gave a dark yet nervous chuckle. "Yeah, I – I'm foreign. *Very*... foreign. It's complicated."

Helga shook her head. "I meant no offense, sir. You could come from beyond the great mountains for all I care. You saved my little girl. Thank you a thousand times – again. Please, remember my words if you ever find yourself in need."

"I will." He stepped back, offering a wave with his right hand. "Farewell. And... may your gods bless you too; both of you."

With that, he took his leave. A small taste of serenity touched his soul. Kye took his time wandering back down the streets of Illikon as the city slowly awoke. Sunlight chased away the shadows. Despite the way it made his skin twinge and something deep within him stir in fear, Kye welcomed it.

For, he knew, the darkness would return soon enough. He always dreaded that moment.

He returned to the Flogged Donkey Inn, and the patrons parted for him like they always did. Also like always, he ignored their looks, though they were more incredulous than before given the blood on his person. He ascended the stairs two at a time, rounding the corner for the tiny room he and Niall had occupied for the last few nights.

Inside, Niall sat behind the room's one meager table, a pile of coins under his nose. Gold coins, no less – Imperial *aurei*, extremely valuable in Achaea and beyond, a currency that held its worth even in foreign lands, thanks to its purity. Kye pushed the door shut with his foot, his eyes on the precious coins that glimmered tantalizingly in the light of Niall's single candle.

Niall's black gaze cut his way. "These are mine," he snapped. "Don't get any ideas."

"I wasn't," Kye replied innocently; naturally, he had been getting all sorts of ideas. "Where'd you get so much money?

Did you mug somebody moving coin from the treasury? Things like that will get us noticed, too."

"No. That would be stupid. I see you're suddenly pleased with yourself; I preferred when you moped and fretted and brooded quietly in a corner."

Kye made a face at him but insisted, "Where'd you get the gold, Niall?"

"None of your business."

"Like it or not, we're partners. It *is* my business."

"Fine. *You* may not have taken anything of value from the Pelagius home during our visit – you thought only of your sword and that ridiculous toy – but I did."

Silence fell. Every shadow in the room seemed to elongate. Kye stared. Realizations crashed down around him like toppling walls.

"*You...*" he snarled.

Niall looked up from the coins, fear invading his face. "I did nothing to deserve this reaction," he blurted.

Kye surged to his feet. Niall started so badly his knees hit the underside of the flimsy desk, sending his coins flying. Two heavy steps, and Kye bore down on the desk, pinning Niall against the wall where he sat.

"You *stole that tome!*" Kye roared. "You— you took it and pawned it off to some other thoughtless fool who knows nothing of what it contains – of the *evil* inside it! *That's* what the knight sensed! It wasn't *me*; it was that book about demons – and he sensed where we were because *you had the damned thing!*"

Niall remained frozen.

Kye swore in a demonic tongue. Speaking it aloud made darkness press so hard against the meager candlelight it nearly shut it out altogether.

"I *knew* it wasn't me he sensed— I knew no one here can do that! Ahriman's blood!" Kye gripped the desk harder, his claws making the wood creak in protest. "You're why we got *caught!*"

"*Almost* got caught," Niall corrected in a tiny voice.

Kye gnashed his teeth, not realizing he had fangs once again, nor realizing his tail lashed behind him and his eyes had turned violet. "I should kill you. Always you reek of more sins than I can count. Mortals should never learn of demons— no good comes of it. Your entire *world* suffers! But you don't care, all because you got a pittance of coin!"

"This is hardly a pittance—"

Kye's left hand shot for Niall's throat, but Niall was faster. He held aloft a heavy medallion of a crescent moon with clouds passing over it: a holy symbol of Nyx, primordial titan, personification of night itself – and still a goddess, no matter how ancient.

Candlelight winked off the bronze emblem, reflecting on Kye's face. Terror rushed into his soul. Ice dropped into his stomach and coursed through his veins, claws of cold fear grasping his heart. Divine power pulled the strength from his very limbs and left pain behind. A deep, inhuman growl like the rumbling of an otherworldly beast sounded in Kye's throat, reverberating off the walls.

He recoiled, shielding his face behind his gauntlet. He cowered and sank low, eyes pinched shut. His spaded tail thumped pathetically on the floor like it writhed in pain.

Niall rose from the chair, still holding the symbol. Kye didn't move.

"I know what you did on that ship," said Niall. "You gave in to the evil inside you, only just enough. The gods frighten that blood of yours. When you are not performing such...

deeds, I've even seen you walk in temples, as you did in Coronaria. But, right now, I'm not sure you could even do that. You are too much of a monster. A demon."

Kye whimpered – a very human sound, unlike before. He couldn't move, or at least he dared not. His limbs felt locked in place. He didn't fight it.

"It's what you *really* are," Niall continued calmly. "Having a human mother doesn't make you human... and having a soul doesn't make you benevolent. I know what you can become, if you but stopped fighting. It's what you *will* become, someday. A *true* demon. I saw it in that book. The power you wield is incredible, and I know this. I even respect it. But if you harm me, Kye, the Messengers will turn on you – and you'll be alone. Remember what it was to be alone?"

Swallowing, Kye bowed his head. "I'm... I'm sorry," he said, his voice low.

"Not good enough, Kye." Niall held the holy symbol closer. Tingling rose in Kye's flesh. He scooted back an inch, but Niall followed, bidding him be still. "How much farther would I have to push you to see what you *really* look like? To finally see you lose all semblance of this false human visage?"

Kye kept his eyes shut, kneeling, unmoving.

"You know what might happen, yet you defy the Silent Messengers. I'll forgive you this once, since I know your blood is still up. This behavior from you is unusual... and it must never happen again. Let this be a reminder: demon or cambion, human blood or no, you are a monster, Kye. *No one* of this world will take you in, save us. Those who desire power would enslave you. Those who follow goodness would slay you. Only the Messengers have given you a home, made you an equal. Never forget that you are an assassin of our order, Kye Vakurseth..."

Kye cringed and bowed his head even lower.

"...and that you are a *coward*. I have seen *this*, as well. You never would've stopped Faro nor saved the girl if you hadn't acted out of fear— fear of losing your father's gift. Would he have punished you for losing that sword, when you inevitably go back to him? Is that what drove you so hard? Like why you saved the girl, trying to reclaim even a shred of the humanity you lost during your battle?"

Silence.

"Now," Niall finished, retracting the holy symbol, "stand."

Not lowering his gauntlet, Kye arose, though he hunched low in defeat.

"Stop hiding your face. It's embarrassing."

Kye's hand dropped. He opened his eyes, his gaze fixed firmly on the floor. The two assassins remained motionless before, finally, Niall tucked the holy symbol away again.

"We must resume the search for our target," he said. "Your defiance has lasted long enough. When our work here is complete, the Messengers will hear of your actions, and I'll let them judge you. I have no doubt they'll let you stay, Kye, but if you're smart, you will never again act as you did here."

Kye nodded.

Niall threw his hand out in dismissal. "Look human again, demon. We're leaving, and Men such as I were not meant to gaze upon such a thing as you."

Kye grated out but a few words, uttering, "*Don't*... call me 'demon.'"

"Cambion. Whatever. I care nothing for your semantics, for a demon is what you are. If you hate 'demon' and 'monster' so, then I'll call you 'beast.'"

Throwing his cloak over his shoulders, the long black cape trailing behind him, Niall led the way from the room. Kye followed in cowed silence. What a fool he was...

They returned to the open streets and the beautiful sunlight of a fine Illikon morning – and went to take the life of an honorable man.

On the way to the Monument District, Kye observed more and more pedestrians heading for Illikon's main street, the one running directly from the eastern gate to the castle. Silently, he drifted in that direction, and Niall followed. They soon arrived at the scene of countless Illikon citizens and some apparent refugees from beyond Coldstone Wall, from Northrim itself, once more lining the streets. All eyes watched a procession of knights on horseback that entered through the city's main gate...

Kye saw their target immediately.

Atop a horse, Sir Tom Drake looked as large and intimidating as ever. He wore a hard scowl, and though he didn't wear his horsehair helmet from before, he still towered over the riders around him. His armor was battered, as was the man himself, but it stole no fire from his bright green eyes— eyes set upon someone near the head of the procession.

Kye followed his target's gaze to a heavily-armored knight on horseback. On his chest was emblazoned the multi-pointed star of the Paladins of the Achaean Empire. He was surely someone important, though Kye had never seen him before, nor did he care... but something caught his eye – a gauntlet on the knight's left hand. It didn't belong on a mortal. Made of dark steel, it ended in claws, though they were much shorter than Kye's own. Still, it reminded him disturbingly of his own gauntlet, yet he knew it couldn't possibly have been the same. Kye pried his attention from the head paladin, however.

Between glares at the lead paladin, Drake kept looking at a woman bound on horseback, a smattering of deep green war paint on her much-exposed bare skin – a warrior-woman, tall and strong, not at all like the civilized and well-dressed women of the Empire. She was clearly a Nordling, with a long blond braid over her shoulder and her hands tied to the saddle of the horse she rode against her will. Kye watched her. She was beautiful...

The procession made their way down the street uninterrupted, everyone parting for them and gazing in awe at the knights and Paladins and their apparent prisoner of war, whom they brandished like a trophy despite her being a woman. Kye wondered about all of it, but he couldn't let it concern him. His only concern wore armor covered in red dragons – and seemed determined to keep pace with the Paladins and their warrior woman prisoner.

Drake looked furious. Bloodthirsty. From the way he kept glaring at the Paladin, Kye figured he wasn't likely to obey orders, particularly where the beautiful prisoner was concerned. Which, she *was* very pretty, so he didn't blame the knight—

Niall pulled him from staring at the Nordling woman. "Well," Kye's partner said under his breath, "there is certainly no reaching him right now. We must lay a trap for him at his home and not balk this time."

"No," Kye replied, half in thought. His eyes drifted toward Castle Illikon in the distance, its mighty towers reaching high. "I don't think he's going home. But I have an idea..."

THE STORY CONTINUES

in...

The Prophecy of the Six, Book I:

KNIGHTFALL

WULFGARD: KNIGHTFALL PREVIEW

- CHAPTER II -
The Dragon's Wrath

Tom led the way as he, Valens, and Corben left Castle Illikon. Behind them loomed the massive keep and the high stone walls protecting the castle grounds, the enormous wooden drawbridge lowered during times of peace. Sundown approached, and although the feast was still going strong, Tom was eager to escape. Naturally, his friends joined him.

Gazing long upon the castle behind them, Tom took a deep breath full of pride. Castle Illikon was one of the most striking in the Empire, built as a symbol of Imperial glory in the wild and untamed north. Its turrets reached for the stars, and from them fluttered Illikon's deep blue banners with the golden gryphon. Seated on the brink of a high cliff coastline, several turrets jutted over the sea, as if suspended in midair above the waves. Of course, that was on the opposite side of the castle and could only be seen by ship, but Tom loved it from any view.

He also loved the city around them. The distant murmur of voices from the streets, the clopping of horses' hooves on the cobblestones, the creaking of cart wheels – these sounds were like music to his ears after standing so long in a room of tittering nobles.

Valens and Corben walked in tow behind him, though they weren't lost in Illikon's undying beauty like Tom. They looked at the sky in a way that told they thought only about the hour instead. A few stars already twinkled in the growing darkness.

Valens said as they walked, "Well, I should leave for Rimegard. It'll be a long ride."

There it was again: Rimegard, the largest city north of Illikon and the only considerable Imperial city beyond Coldstone Wall. That wall stood as the barrier between the Northwestern Kingdom of Illikon and the untamed wilderness of Northrim, where Rimegard was the lone bastion of Imperial civilization. Tom had been there before, though it was quite the long journey. He even knew the Princess of Rimegard, Adrianna Skiera. She was a friend and a good one, plus she was a niece to Queen Carlisa Illikoni.

Tom frowned. "Already? Is it really that bad up there?"

Valens shrugged and stopped walking; the others followed his example. "Not sure. It does sound like it's gotten worse... I wish I could stay for the rest of the tournament, but orders are orders. I'll be back in a couple weeks, I hope."

"Don't die up there, Valens," said Corben. "And don't freeze to death."

Valens laughed, though it held little mirth. "I'm not going *that* far north."

Tom pulled Valens into a hug, then drew back and clapped him on the shoulder. "If you *do* die, you'll never hear the end of it. I'll see you in a few weeks, Val. Be careful – and don't get walked all over without me to stick up for you."

"I'm a lot more worried about *you*, Tom." He gave Corben a pleading look. "Keep him out of trouble."

"Aye, like anybody can do that," Corben muttered.

"I know. Farewell, both of you."

With a brief wave, Valens strode off. Tom and Corben watched him leave. For a while, they stayed silent, only sharing a worried look.

"D'you actually believe Marks?" Corben asked at length. "About not tryin' to hurt you in the joust?"

Tom gave a laugh and a one-sided grin. "Are you kidding me? No."

"What, you don't trust his word? Ain't he a knight?"

"Doesn't mean he has to act like one."

"Straight from the horse's mouth..."

Tom shrugged. "At least I'm honest."

"Aye, chivalrous, too. Certainly are generous to the women."

"Little below the belt, there, Cor."

"Literally."

"Oho, that's *really* funny. Talk about your simple humor."

Their walk took them to the northern district of Illikon called the Monument District, named such for its many statues of gods and heroes, where most of the noble families owned expensive manors. Tom always felt odd stepping into this district with the intention of going home, even after all these years.

He and his friends rarely spoke of it, but they all knew Tom's true heritage as half Nordling, a bastard son of a noble Drake and a 'barbarian' woman he'd met on a campaign. What happened to his mother, Tom still had no idea, but he knew his father died shortly after Tom's birth. Disowned by the Drakes at first, Tom grew up on the streets, stealing to survive, before Earl Warren finally took him in.

The popular assumption was that Warren adopted him so he could raise his own male heir with family blood. He only had daughters, himself. Such spelled the end for an ancient Achaean house.

Their arrival at the sprawling Drake household pulled Tom from his thoughts. Outside the gate waited Lady Severina Kallistos, clad in an elaborate green and blue gown, her long auburn hair hanging loose. To Tom, she looked particularly beautiful with the Draconius manor's intricate High Imperial architecture in the background. Columns surrounded the house, its walls covered in designs of dragons and historic battles. Two massive dragon statues flanked the main gate, rearing on their hind legs like Tom's sigil.

Severina smiled at him, and Tom smiled back. His expression earned him a snort from Corben.

"Seems you got *company*, Tom," Corben commented in a ridiculously suggestive tone, as he readjusted the cone helmet he'd since donned.

Tom rapped his knuckles on said helmet, making Corben jerk away. He then approached Severina, calling over his shoulder, "See you tomorrow, Cor."

"Aye," Corben replied blandly before walking off.

Tom took Severina's hand and gave her fingers a kiss. "No hard feelings about that joust, right?" he asked with one of his usual charming smiles.

"Not *this* time," replied Severina. "Gnaeus had it coming."

"Can't disagree there," Tom said, opening the gate to the manor. The two started walking.

"Hopefully *you* don't have any hard feelings about what Gnaeus said," she added. "He can be a lout sometimes. He listens to Cassian too much."

"Yeah, I'm used to that. I got nothing against him. He apologized, and besides, a lot of people listen to Cassian. He's probably one of the most respected knights in the city. Hell if I know why."

Severina nodded and fell quiet. Tom frowned. She wasn't exactly the talkative type, but the suddenness of the silence worried him.

Finally, she said, "We need to talk, Tom."

Tom stopped, looking into her earthy brown-green eyes. He knew he was no good at reading people, as Valens so often pointed out, but something troubled her. If nothing else, he heard it in her tone.

"Sure thing," he said. "About what?"

Severina glanced at a nearby servant on the grounds. Her eyes flicked back to him, pointedly.

And she said, "In private."

While not the largest room, Tom's quarters were certainly accommodating. Frescos of dragons and legendary heroes decorated the walls alongside maps of both faraway places and the Northwestern Kingdom itself, the realm of Illikon. Armor stands occupied several corners, one such stand bearing Tom's battle armor: sleeveless muscle cuirass, horsehair helmet, boots, and bracers forged in the style of an Imperial hoplite, including a tasset belt. Unlike true hoplites, however, Tom wore trousers into battle with this armor – like a barbarian.

Weapon racks decorated the room as well. Swords and axes lined much of the space, every one kept in pristine condition. Hanging among them but bearing special importance was Tom's war-horn, decorated in red dragons and golden gryphons. Its call was recognized across the Empire and Northrim, but Tom had never used it. Such horns only saw use in warfare, and despite his experiences in skirmishes and other fights and battles, Tom had yet to see true war.

Lastly, Tom's bed was large, soft, and luxurious, colored entirely red and gold and nestled between a pair of windows. Rather than a romantic sunset, however, the dim light of a dreary evening filled the space. The sky had become overcast, and rain pattered on the roof. It ran down the expensive glass windows, blurring the beautiful view of Illikon and the sea.

Severina entered his room first, glancing it over. As her gaze crossed the frescos and weapons, she shook her head.

"You've added things since I was here last," she remarked. "It certainly speaks to your interests."

Tom shut the door with his foot and said coyly, "Does it?"

Severina looked at the rug under their feet, which was soft, red and gold, and from a distant far southern land. She nodded and replied, "Definitely."

He grinned. "I'll take that as a compliment. I'll bet yours doesn't look so different."

She chuckled. "Much to my mother's dismay. Though thankfully it isn't quite this exotic."

But she kept her back to him. Tom paused a moment before moving in front of her, blocking her view of the gloom outside.

"You wanted to talk?" he prompted gently.

"I did. I want to talk about us."

Tom waited, doubting all the while that meant anything good, but she didn't say a word. It didn't take long for her to avert her eyes and look frustrated. Tom put a hand on her shoulder and ran his fingers through her long, red-brown hair. It was beautiful, even luxurious, especially for a lady who'd fought so hard to become a knight... not that Tom thought of it that way. Severina had never let being a knight stop her from being a lady. No matter how often the Empire at large said women couldn't be knights, she not only rode into battle, but she came home seamlessly beautiful and ladylike. Only her tan and scars, which she left visible in her choice of dress, told of her knighthood.

"Tell me what's wrong," he said softly.

She shrugged, still not looking at his face. "Nothing's *wrong*, just..."

Her voice drifted, and he quirked a brow. "Yeah it is," he said. "You're worried about something. You won't even look at me, and I know you like looking at me." Tom paused for a reaction, but she neither laughed nor admonished him, which was unusual. "What is it?"

Hesitantly, she looked him in the eye again. She took a breath – but she only frowned.

"I don't know," she said abruptly. "I don't know... how to put it."

"Something to do with Cassian?"

"You could say that."

"If this has to do with that whole ladies' man thing..."

"It does and it doesn't. Not directly. I'd always guessed that, but I know you're a good man. I don't care about Cassian's rumors."

"Okay... Then what?"

She went quiet again. Tom's fingers wandered down her hair to her collarbone, sliding across a scar there and sneaking over her shoulder. All the while, he kept watching her and worrying. Severina put a hand on the back of his neck before he could speak again, pulling just enough to indicate she wanted him closer. He complied – and kissed Severina on the lips.

She pulled him closer still, wrapping her other arm around him. Her hips pressed into his. He slid his hands along her back, finding the fastenings of her bodice, but she leaned her head back enough to look at him. Reluctantly – very reluctantly – he stopped.

"I hate to ask it like this, but..." she started.

Tom nuzzled at her cheek and intoned, "Hm?"

"Is that a dagger in your pocket?"

"Maybe I'm just..." he began instantly, but Severina reached into said pocket and drew a sheathed dagger that had been pressed against his leg. Tom grunted pointedly.

"Stop being a smartass for *one minute*," she said as she tried to slip away from him. Tom didn't let her, but he gave an inch or two of space, resting his chin on her head.

"One whole minute," he replied. "I promise."

"What is this?"

Tom shrugged, still not releasing her. "You're right. It's a dagger. What's it look like, a—?"

"Promise, remember?"

He cleared his throat. "Alright."

"You carried this to the *banquet?*"

"So? There were plenty of knives around."

"Dinner knives and carving knives, not weapons."

"Anything's a weapon if you try hard enough."

"Stop it. Don't tell me you were planning to stab Cassian Marks."

"Stab? No, I was just going to cut him a little bit. It'd probably *improve* his face. Man looks like a muscular toddler who stuck on a fake beard – a few scars would do him good."

Severina freed her head from under his chin and glared at him. Tom put on his best innocent smile.

"Sev, you think I'm serious?" He finally moved one hand off her back to take the dagger and toss it away. It hit the rich carpet under their feet with a muffled thud. "Look, it's just in case. I grew up in streets and alleys, and out there you *always* carry a knife. I guess old habits die hard."

"You and your fighting... But I can't blame you. Even when I know everyone else is unarmed, or they're *supposed* to be, I still feel naked without a blade."

A smile pulled at Tom's lips. He asked sweetly, "My minute isn't up yet, is it?"

She gave a laugh. "No, it's not, and thank Poseidon for that – even if you've broken it a few times anyway."

Again she squirmed in his arms, and Tom let her go in spite of himself. She straightened her elaborate green and blue dress.

"I should go," Severina said. "I need to get out of this damned dress. Even my armor is more comfortable."

"You look great, if it's any consolation," Tom remarked, meandering behind her. "It's very... elaborate. You probably had help getting it on."

Severina threw him a look as he circled her. He grinned, his teeth glinting in the sparse light. Towering behind her, he leaned his head over one of her shoulders. His fingers slid between her exposed shoulder-blades.

Tone sultry, Tom asked, "Want some help getting it back off?"

She hummed in mock thought and faced him again, pretending to be unaffected by his heady charms. "I might... But only if you aren't clumsy."

Tom reached around to her back and undid her bodice with a few well-practiced tugs. Her dress flowed off her like water and onto the floor. Tom ran his hands over her firmly toned body, his nimble fingers exploring a few scars along the way.

He said, "You know I'm not."

Severina answered by kissing him again. A needy growl sounded in his throat as she slipped her hands under his tunic, sliding a gentle touch up along his ribs to his chest. He all but ripped his tunic off, tossing it in a random direction while she deftly undid his belt. Her concentration impressed him, given he kissed her the entire time.

He pulled her close, but she escaped the kissing and pressed her face against his neck. She purred into his skin, "Neither am I."

Castle Illikon's highest turret overlooked the ocean cliffs on one side and the plains on the other. Tom had never set foot atop it until now. Deep blue roofs capped several turrets of the castle, forming conical points rather than platforms, but this one remained open to the wind.

Emerging from the stairwell's total darkness, Tom stepped into bright light under a full moon. Fear bit the back of his neck. The sensation of being chased crawled over his skin like the night's own chill. He had no time to admire the beauty of the view nor listen to the crashing waves against the shore far below – somehow, he had to find escape. But despite his uncharacteristic terror, when he looked back at the trapdoor, he saw nothing.

He spun in place, searching, knowing he'd cornered himself. He knew not what chased him, only that something did, and it terrified him. Almost nothing frightened him, but whatever pursued him put the fear of death deep in his heart like no battle or even a demon from another world ever had.

Not even he could fight so irrational a fear as what overwhelmed him now.

Frigid wind blew, howling and whistling, striking him with such force he nearly staggered. It was so strong that he felt a need to reach a battlement and hold on, so he didn't lose his footing—

It found him.

Eyes set upon him. Tom sensed it. Wheeling, he watched a nightmare emerge from the trapdoor, rising to meet him. Yet, as it did, shadows passed over the full moon and cast everything in darkness.

Animal eyes, blue as ice, watched him through the blackness. A huge shape straightened itself, unfolding from the small space of the stairwell, bound in muscle and greater in size than any man. And it was... wrong. All wrong. Its shape was not entirely human, nor was its head – a head like a beast. Like a wolf. Sparse moonlight glinted off silver-white fur, an animal hide on a nearly human body...

The wind struck again. Tom stood his ground, planting his feet against it. The beast, with arms and hands like a man's but with long fingers ending in wicked claws, remained motionless and silhouetted against the night. Untouched by nature's power, the wind did nothing to the wolf-man.

But Tom couldn't stand against it. Harder it came, a gale from beyond Northrim itself. The breath of the very gods moved him in place, his boots sliding against the stone underfoot, carrying him toward the edge. Deafening, wind filled his ears. Tom brought his arms before his face, hunkering his tall form low – but it didn't matter.

He slid until his hip struck the battlements. They broke beneath his weight like brittle sticks rather than stone. Tom grasped for a hold but found nothing. Air rushed around him, stung his eyes, filled his ears, his heart racing – and he toppled from the tower, plummeting into nothing. A fall that spelled certain death...

Tom awoke with a jolt – as if from the finality of impact.

The sensation of falling remained with him a moment longer, but his own dark bedroom greeted his open eyes. Thunder resounded off the stone walls. White lightning flashed and made him blink. Beside him, Severina scrambled awake at his disturbance.

"What?" she said breathlessly. "Tom, what's wrong?"

Swallowing, Tom sat up and gathered his senses. Storms had rolled off the sea, only growing worse as the night wore on. Rain now dashed against the stone manor and the window-glass, the ruckus filling Tom's ears, which felt unusually sensitive. Lightning again lit the room, reflecting in Tom's shining armor on its stand. Maybe the storm had given him such an absurd nightmare. That made some kind of sense, didn't it? Why would he dream about some twisted man-wolf when he'd never seen nor heard of such a thing?

Finally, Tom answered, "Just... had a bad dream. A very strange bad dream." He forced a small laugh, realizing how childish he sounded. "It's, ah – it's nothing. Sorry I woke you."

"It's fine. But a lot of people would tell you that dreams are visions and you shouldn't ignore them. Even the Nordlings believe that, I think."

"I've never seen anything like what was in the dream. It's just nonsense."

Severina frowned, and Tom knew his voice had betrayed too much concern. "And yet it bothered you. What did you see?"

"I... I don't know, like I said. It made no sense – it wasn't something that'd actually *happen*. Besides, I don't have 'visions.' I probably just drank too much at the feast."

They spoke no more. Tom settled back down, but Severina slipped away not long after, taking with her the comforting warmth of another body against his own. She lay motionless against the bed's head, listening to the ripping rain. Tom followed her gaze to a fresco of a great red dragon. Its features came to life with each flash of lightning. Severina watched it as if it watched her back, critically.

"Tom," she said at length, "can I ask you something?"

His eyes never left her, for he knew from the gravity of her voice she no longer thought of his nightmare. He answered, "You know you can."

Severina sighed and leaned toward him. Tom rested his chin on her head again. Without a word, she tucked her face against his throat for a while before finally responding.

"I've been... thinking about those rumors Cassian keeps spreading."

Tom frowned. "Are his rumors really that important? Didn't you say you didn't care?"

"We're knights, Tom. We shouldn't even be together *right now*, nor should we ever until it's formal. We've got reputations to maintain."

"Especially you," Tom finished for her, his voice low.

"Yes... especially me. This concept of dames, 'lady-knights,' we have so many names now – it leaves me scrutinized. Most of the Empire considers it foolish, barbaric, and weak. Women have no place in battle. Sometimes, I'm not sure they're wrong, and when I think that, I compare myself to the shield-maidens of Northrim... which *does* make it barbaric."

"And you're worried about being with someone like me. Someone with a bad reputation."

Severina didn't answer.

"Look, *some* of what he's saying is probably true. I don't know all of it, so I can't really deny every single accusation."

"The fact that you're with me right now – and that I'm with you – is a confirmation of some, at least. For us both."

"Who gives a damn?"

"That's another thing he says, that you talk like a commoner and that it's demeaning to all nobility."

"The f—"

"Like that," she cut in.

"In my defense, I also curse in other *languages*, which shows how smart I am."

"Tom."

"Fine, I get it. So the," he gestured vaguely with one hand, "review. I'm not dumb, Sev. You're leading up to something – go ahead and say it."

Severina shifted against him, but she didn't make a sound. Blood rose in Tom's face.

"I don't *want* to say it," she said. "I don't want to *do* it, either."

"But you're going to. Right? You're gonna break off this relationship before it hurts your shiny dame reputation – before it can go anywhere." He was talking when he knew he shouldn't. "Because when it all comes down to it, I'm still just that scruffy bastard-son half-barbarian street rat everybody wants to keep on a chain."

She leaned away, looking him in the face. "It's not like that, Tom," Severina said, slowly and gravely. "I care for you. But us being together... I'm not sure it's right."

"Oh, to hell with *'right,'* Severina!" Tom blurted before he could stop himself. "What do you wanna do, go marry someone like Cassian Marks? Because *he's* so upstanding, right?"

She sighed. "I've been thinking about this for a while," she admitted quietly. "It's not Cassian. But every time I get ready to do it, you pull me in again... Just like tonight."

Tom said nothing.

At length, she offered weakly, "I'm sorry. I'm not blaming you for any of this, Tom. But... we can't do this anymore."

Tom only intoned a low, "Yeah." After a moment, he added, "I'm sorry too."

Frustration burned in his chest, but with that, Severina got out of bed. Tom didn't look at her while she gathered her things and escaped.

When the door thudded shut, Tom slumped onto the pillows.

Thick grey clouds veiled the sun the next day. Corben McShane whistled absent-mindedly, waiting outside the Draconius manor and watching servants bustle about. He had met Severina in the streets a few hours ago. He'd assumed Tom would leave for the castle as well now that she was gone, yet Corben still saw no sight of him.

Severina had seemed troubled, but Corben doubted he read her right. Beautiful women, he thought, were hard to read and even harder to understand. Sometimes, he considered himself glad he didn't have one. Curse Tom. How'd he ever get so lucky?

A horse's nicker at his back interrupted his thoughts, and Tom said gruffly, "Surprised to see *you* here."

Corben regarded Tom Drake, who sat atop his sheer black stallion, the horse's white forehead star shining prominently right in Corben's face. Ghost was not yet garbed in his tournament attire. The steed snorted, sharing his rider's annoyance. Tom wore a stony expression, much to Corben's surprise.

Corben raised a brow. "For a fella who just spent the night with a lovely lady, you don't seem too happy."

"Always direct, huh, Cor?"

"Aye. Well, shouldn't you be chipper?"

"Not exactly."

He set Ghost off at a walk, forcing Corben to step aside and allow the horse passage. Tom's frustration made Corben hesitate, wondering, before he hurried alongside his friend's stallion.

"Why not, then?" asked Corben. Arrogant smiles, cheerful comments, and dry remarks generally flew this way and that after Tom had spent a night with Severina. "Severina left you, didn't she?"

Tom visibly clenched his jaw before answering, "Apparently being one of the only lady knights in the Northwest cost us our relationship. She didn't want to jeopardize what little respect she gets." Tom shook his head. "I know what she's going through better than most, but..."

"But *you* wouldn't let somethin' like your 'reputation' stand in the way o' something or someone you really care about. Batty noble women... You're too good for 'em, Tom."

"I might not care much about *my* reputation," Tom said, "but I care about hers. It's very important to her. I just didn't think I was endangering it. I wouldn't *want* to. I know she works hard on her knighthood."

"I guess she was worried people might talk about it more, with all these rumors flyin' around... Anyway, you'll feel better once you kick Marks's arse, right?"

Tom's eyes wandered. "Maybe a *little*."

"You will. An' I guess I'm your help now that Magnus left. Can't wait to see all the looks the nobs are gonna give me."

They approached the castle gates now, and Corben wondered what he was doing. He didn't belong in a world of knights and nobles – he belonged among taverns, common soldiers, thieves, and sailors. Fellow watchmen, smelly drinking buddies, and long hours – it was uglier, but at least it was a trifle more honest. Tom, meanwhile, lived at once in and between both worlds, like some kind of double life. Why couldn't Tom get another squire?

"Just give them right back," Tom replied, sounding grim rather than cheerful. "I'll back you up."

Corben chuckled, feeling better. Given Tom's low mood, however, he said no more on their way to the lists.

Crisp rain freshened the humid air, and a fine drizzle created a thin but foreboding mist. Yet no rain could dampen the colorful pavilions against the green tourney grounds, especially Tom's bright red tent. Neither did the weather dampen the Marks family tent, which had replaced the Kallistos one from before. Yellow and blue stripes ran down the cloth, highlighted by silver bands. Flags bearing the Marks crest of blue fishes on a yellow field hung damply from their poles with hardly a breeze livening them.

Despite the rain, the spectator turnout impressed and troubled Corben. Every important face was present, joined by many lesser-known figures besides – not that Corben knew his nobility very well. The stands looked full to bursting, and several more spectators lurked along the far edges of the green, even with joust coordinators warning them back. Corben noticed Tom tighten his grip on Ghost's reins.

"Looks like they're itchin' to see who'll win this little feud," Corben said darkly. "Even though it supposedly ain't a feud, which I don't think *anybody* believes. Else maybe they're so paranoid o' what's supposedly goin' on in Northrim that they don't know where else to be."

"I just hope Marks keeps his word," Tom replied. Glancing Corben's way, he remarked, "You're gonna take that dorky thing off before we joust, right?"

Corben chuckled and removed his dome helmet. "Let's get you suited up."

Steadier rain pinged on Tom's armor as he halted Ghost in the field. Through the steel teeth of his dragon helm, he saw Cassian Marks, clad in his own colorful scale hauberk, opposite him on the long lists. Fins adorned Marks's helm, his yellow plume with a silver stripe in the center drooping in the rain. Every inch of Cassian's armor carried motifs of fins, ocean waves, and fish, not unlike the dragon theme Tom wore. Alongside Cassian's horse, his young squire passed Cassian a targe and a yellow-and-silver striped lance.

"Do us all a favor and don't kill him, alright, Tom?" Corben said, helping Tom strap a bright red shield onto his arm.

Tom laughed and took the lance next. "What, did you promise Val you'd nag me? I took an oath, Cor, same as the oath I took to defend Illikon herself. Believe it or not, I take those very seriously."

"Aye, I know the spill 'bout you being a man of your word. I hope he's feelin' the same way." Corben looked at Cassian, who waited in silence atop his chestnut charger wearing its colorful caparison. Cassian's great helm entirely covered his face, with only the narrowest of slits for eye-holes, making him look far from merciful.

Tom said, "He'll regret it if he doesn't."

Corben rolled his eyes. Trumpets split the air before Tom could drop another remark, and Corben moved directly into Tom's vision yet again. The watchman's earth-green eyes betrayed his worry.

"Don't do somethin' stupid," Corben said gravely, in the same tone one might use when seeing someone stand at the edge of a cliff—which Tom had done before and been lectured less.

Denying Tom a retort, Corben dashed off, joining Cassian's squire near the audience stands. The boy stood much shorter than Corben, but he held his nose much higher.

Even from his distance, Tom heard every word when they spoke.

"How you doin', boy?" Corben said with a friendly smile.

The boy screwed up his brow. "You're awfully common for a squire. And *old*."

"Your nanny didn't beat you enough, did she? Watch your lip unless you want me to fix her mistake."

The boy fell silent, and Tom stopped listening, though he hoped Cassian's squire didn't tell his master about Corben's disrespect. But Tom's attention quickly turned elsewhere. His blood was up; he could feel it. His heart thudded too hard in his chest, his lust for battle beating strong once again. Sensing it, Ghost pawed at the ground. Tom tensed, tightened his grip on his lance, and let Ghost shoot straight ahead at full gallop.

Wind and rain cut into his thin visor like a knife. Tom squinted against it, taking aim and focusing only on the blue fish in the center of Cassian's targe...

Impact rattled him in the saddle. The lances snapped.

The knights' weapons shattered against each other in a resounding *crack* and an explosion of splinters. Neither reached their targets. Tom released the broken lance as his horse kept running, stopping only when he reached the other side of the tilt.

De-horsing the other knight often didn't happen. Tom knew that, yet he always aimed for it regardless, for his eternal aim was to give more of a spectacle, a better show of his strength and skill. Every time it didn't happen, he only grew angrier.

Corben grabbed a new lance off a nearby rack and ambled over to meet him. Silently, Tom repositioned Ghost opposite the tilt while runners fetched the lance splinters, removing them from the field. As relatively new a sport as jousting was for the Empire, they had it down to an art already.

"How's it goin'?" asked Corben as he fitted another lance into Tom's waiting, gauntleted hand.

"I was hoping I'd dismount him on the first pass," Tom answered.

"Aye, well, if wishes were horses, then maybe *I'd* be ridin' one today. You'll get him before you know it."

Again the clarion trumpets sounded, and Corben nodded before retreating. Tom once more focused only on Cassian as everyone else cleared the field.

"Let's finish this," Tom muttered, aiming his lance across Ghost's neck.

Again the steeds streaked across the grassy field, becoming little more than colorful red and gold or yellow and blue blurs in the rain – blurs carrying riders distinguished by colors and helms, Tom's horns and Cassian's plume. Heaviness filled the air already so overburdened with tension. Every spectator leaned forward. They neared again...

But the lances glanced off their targets.

The horses stopped on opposite sides of the field. Half the audience jeered. Tom cast a glance up at them, rainwater running down the snout of his dragon helm and dripping from its various hornlets and spikes.

"They're as tired of this as I am," Tom remarked.

Corben checked his lance but said, "I thought you lived for this kinda stuff, Tom. Just relax. He'll slip sooner or later."

"Slip?" Tom laughed. "What, you think he's as good as I am?"

Frowning, Corben leaned closer. His tone changed when he said, "Don't get too cocky. I mean it. Marks wasn't playin' around at that banquet."

Tom just laughed again. "Don't be so dramatic, Cor. I'll deal with Cassian Marks, and you can take care of his squire."

Corben's gravity turned into confusion. "You heard what I said to the boy? From all the way over here, and in that wild helmet?"

"Technically it's a 'helm,'" Tom replied ribbingly.

The trumpets sounded again, louder than ever, nearly splitting Tom's head wide open. The signal to charge had come again, yet Corben still looked concerned, as if he watched a knight plot murder.

Tom gestured him away with his shield arm, his levity spent. "Look, I told you I'm not gonna hurt him. Now get back where it's safe – I don't think Cassian would care if he trampled you."

Corben finally retreated, and Tom refocused for the third time. The rain had slowed again, giving a clearer view of the field and his adversary.

The horses charged. Tom leaned low over Ghost's neck, shield close at his side. Gracefully, he lowered his lance into position. Cassian neared, closer and closer – and again Tom took aim, bracing himself for whatever impact awaited...

The point of a lance stared right at him. Cassian's lance was aimed high. *Too* high. It was aimed right at his—

Pain exploded into Tom's head. Wood splintered everywhere, impact rattling his teeth. His ears rang. He wasn't in the saddle anymore – he wasn't anywhere for what felt like several seconds.

Then his back slammed hard against the ground, knocking the wind from his lungs. Everything hurt, his head spun, and something hot and sticky ran down his face. Tom swore in at least four languages, though only in his mind. He lacked the breath to speak.

Cassian had aimed for his head. Worse, he'd aimed for the one weak point in his otherwise impenetrable helm, directly at his visor – at his face.

A beat passed.

Everything kept spinning. Tom's ears rang so loudly he couldn't hear himself think. He didn't move, spread-eagled on the ground, unsure which way was up. A few moments later, he found his senses and stood, grabbing at the air. His hands caught the tilt, the wooden bar separating the two riders on the jousting field. Sucking air back into his chest, Tom leaned against it, freeing his hands to tug off his helm and arming cap. Blinking past blood, he dropped them both.

A long splinter protruded askew from his dragon-maw visor. Blood covered the left side of his head. Hot stickiness coated his face as well, running so profusely it dripped off his chin, the stink filling his nose. He grimaced and pressed a gauntleted hand on his wounded forehead, where still more blood partially matted the angry spikes of his hair.

Corben ran over, but Tom barely noticed. The wild pounding of his heart filled his ears, all but deafening him. A veil of hot red rage dropped over his vision. Through it, he watched Cassian Marks dismount his steed on the opposite side of the lists, his movements casual. Calm. As if everything had gone according to plan, as if satisfied with himself— a man who had given his word to Queen Illikoni and then broken it the very next day.

Tom tore his hand away from his face, his fingers trailing his own blood. He ripped the shield from his arm. Instinctively, he reached for a sword hilt above his shoulder – but they weren't there. Only in his battle armor did he carry his swords on his back, not his tournament gear.

Urgent words reached Tom's ears but not his mind. Corben kept saying something, but Tom didn't listen. When he looked at Corben, all he saw was his sword-belt slung over Corben's shoulder, ready for when the melee started.

Fury silenced Tom's every thought. He straightened despite the blood. Corben froze. He looked frightened. Tom reached over, pulled the belt off Corben's shoulder, and drew his twin blades before Corben registered what had happened.

"Tom, wait!"

Words still couldn't reach Tom Drake. He wasn't listening – he couldn't listen. He heard only his lust for blood.

Tom moved toward his target, head held low like a stalking beast. Spectators stared in alarm. Each step he took made his wrath run hotter, like billows on an inferno, made him grip his swords tighter – and made him pick up the pace.

He cleared the distance of the tilt in seconds. Cassian whirled just before Tom descended on him. Eyes ablaze, gnashing teeth white against the red blood coating his face, Tom let loose a guttural roar that split the pinging rain.

Cassian nearly stumbled in his haste, pulling a sword off the weapon rack behind him. The moment he brought the blade around, Tom's swords were there, slamming into it. The sheer force of Tom's first strike nearly knocked Cassian off his feet.

Cassian's sword-arm moved. Struck at him. Tom swatted it away like a fly.

He kept up the assault, hammering Cassian's shield, as if he wielded a war-hammer instead of a pair of swords. Every time Cassian even twitched to retaliate, Tom deflected it. Instinct told him when Cassian moved, and his speed kept Cassian on the defensive. Tom's blood rushed even faster and stirred a terrible hunger in his soul.

Steel against steel. Steel against wood – wood almost splintering, Cassian's shield weakening. Part of it snapped clean off from Tom's next sword-blow as if deflecting a bull's head-on charge.

Tom didn't register the destruction – didn't register his own strength, his own instinctual precision – and didn't register the desperation in Cassian's every terrified movement. It was weakness, not desperation. Not something he pitied. Only weakness he could exploit.

Behind him, Corben shouted, *"Tom!"*

Still Tom didn't listen. All he knew was Cassian's blood. He wanted to spill it, to smell it so powerfully he tasted it. Cassian kept trying, but he couldn't even get off a swing, not with Tom bearing down on him. Tom made sure of that. He sidestepped Cassian's heaviest swing yet and used it to lunge in, raking a blade across the metal of Cassian's great helm.

That made Cassian stagger, putting him off-balance. Tom saw his chance.

He kicked Cassian so hard in the chest the other knight went flying and slammed hard into the mud. His helm came off his head and bounced across the wet ground. Tom lunged again.

Disable him— Tom slammed a foot onto the wrist of Cassian's sword arm. His other foot landed square on Cassian's chest, pressing hard, crushing the wind from Cassian's lungs and pushing him into the mud.

Hurt him— left sword raised, Tom plunged the blade into Cassian's shoulder between his pauldrons of segmented leather. It went right through his mail like it wasn't even there. Tom earned himself a scream from the squirming knight, a man he no longer recognized. Tom recognized only the scent of blood from Cassian's wound. The hunger in him howled, shutting out everything else. It tightened his rage closer still, every ounce of his vicious focus set on his quarry.

"Drake – Drake, *please!*" begged the knight whose name didn't matter. He shook from head to toe, and his voice shook even worse. "I yield! *I yield!*"

Tom didn't hear him. He pulled his sword from his prey's shoulder. The knight screamed again.

Kill him—

Something slammed into Tom from behind. A pair of strong arms wrapped around Tom's shoulders from underneath to lock his arms above his head.

"Tom, *stop it!*" Corben yelled in his ear. "What the hell's gotten into you!?"

The grip sent pain shooting up Tom's arms, twisting his shoulders. Tom growled and struggled, but it didn't work.

"Let me *go*, Corben!" Tom snarled. "He broke his oath to the Queen – he tried to kill me!"

"Killin' *him* ain't gonna fix that!" Corben shouted back.

Tom didn't answer. He bunched his muscles like an animal and threw a shoulder forward so hard it twisted his arms free from Corben's grip. It also sent his friend sprawling into the mud. Corben landed in a heap, wheezing. One hand gripped his shoulder that had nearly been dislocated.

Suddenly, Tom froze. Corben was his friend. He wouldn't hurt Corben – why had he done that?

Sense slowly seeped back into him. Tom dropped his weapons, his twin swords, Guts and Glory, thudding to the rain-soaked earth.

His heart slowed. His head spun. Pain hit him like a catapult stone, and stars filled his vision. A thousand thoughts that couldn't get through his rage and hunger before now flooded into his mind. With them came pain – so much pain he hadn't felt before. Tom pressed a hand against his skull, realizing the blood on his face had gone all the way down his neck to his scale hauberk. How was he still standing?

As if on cue, his legs gave out. But before the ground met his face, Corben caught him by the arms. From the way Corben buckled and grunted, Tom knew he was incredibly heavy in his gear and not supporting his own weight. As much as he wanted to help Corben, strength had left his limbs, like his body was only just realizing it had been struck a potentially mortal blow.

The world became pulsing blackness and waves of nauseating pain. Thunder rumbled in the distance. Footsteps. Voices – but only a few came through clearly enough to understand.

"I'm sorry..." Cassian sputtered. "I – I didn't mean..."

"Shut up," Corben snapped hotly.

"Get Sir Tom to the healers!" the Queen ordered. "We will deal with his... *outburst* when he is conscious."

Another man came forward and helped Corben carry Tom: Marshal Lucius Fletcher. Tom knew who he was before he even spoke, though he knew not how.

"Dear gods," said Fletcher's voice near Tom's ear. "Let's get him onto a horse. We should hurry. I don't know how he didn't die instantly."

Everything faded rapidly after that, passing into darkness and silence, save for one last sound...

King Aetius's deep voice boomed across the lists, "Take Sir Cassian to the dungeons!"

Tom awoke with a groan. The throbbing in his skull told him he still lived. Warm air touched his skin rather than the cool ground of the rain-soaked lists. He blinked and looked around, finding himself in a long room of stone walls. Candles in golden mounts lit much of the room, though a few small windows between the rows of beds also let in cloud-filtered sunlight. He wasn't in the dungeon, after all. He recognized his surroundings as the house of healing attached to Illikon's temple of Athena.

Sighing, Tom rubbed his aching head. Sticky moistness greeted his fingers, making his stomach do a flip. The blood was gone, but the stained bandages on his head almost reached his left eye. Though they did stop before marring his brow...

Tom let his hand drop, muttering, "At least he didn't mess up my face."

"Aye, might've killed you. Or, worse, ruined your looks."

Corben's voice made Tom start. He sat up, his blurred vision finally focusing on Corben, who sat beside his sickbed, still wearing his same watchman attire from before. Blood stained it in several places. Tom wondered if every drop of it was his own.

"You alright, Tom?" Corben asked. "How many fingers am I holdin' up?"

Tom spared a glance at his hands. "Eight."

Corben looked down at his own fingers and blinked. "Damn, you can count fast."

"I *am* alright, aren't I?" Tom said, poking at the bandage on his head again and wincing with a quiet swear.

"Aye, you'll be fine. You're lucky Marshal Fletcher an' the lady-knight helped me bring you here so fast after you winked out, else you might've ended up worse." Corben leaned back in his chair. "I was surprised you passed out – never seen you pass out before – but then I saw what Marks did to your head. I'm surprised he didn't kill you with what he did. Although maybe I'm even more surprised you didn't kill *him* with what *you* did..."

"As am I," said Cristina Drake as she swept into the room. Cristy was the second oldest of Tom's three adoptive sisters, technically his cousins. Tom didn't give too much thought to his family tree; as far as he was concerned, they were his sisters. He had no other siblings besides, and blood was blood.

She arrived beside his sickbed, all business, as usual. Her long, dark hair was tied up in a bun, and she folded her arms in a way that foretold a scolding.

"Hey, Cristy," Tom said, managing a crooked smile.

"Greetings, Tom," Cristy replied coolly. "Still facing your problems head-on, I see."

Tom made a show of cringing and faked a laugh. "Ahah, that's... *really* funny."

"In all seriousness, Cassian was either trying to kill you or, like Corben said, mess up your face. That lance splinter could easily have pierced your skull. You're lucky his aim wasn't better, and that your helm deflected as much as it did."

Grinning, Tom elbowed Corben. "Pretty good for a lizard with horns."

Corben just sneered.

Cristy smiled. "You have a right to be smug. I don't think lesser men would've survived the blow you *did* receive... but I hate to see you look death so closely in the face, Tom."

"Me too, trust me." Tom rubbed his bandage again. "He's ugly."

Cristy gently took Tom's hand and pushed it away. "Try not to touch it," she warned. "You'll open the wound. It'll leave a scar either way, but you've bled more than enough. I'm fairly certain he *did* crack your skull."

"And people always tell me I have such a thick head. Ah well, maybe it'll let some of the demons out."

"Oh, and... there's somethin' else," said Corben, exchanging glances with Cristina. Tom suddenly felt very uncomfortable. His hand inched toward the silver dragon amulet around his neck. Apparently, whoever had taken off his armor while he was out knew better than to remove the trinket.

"What is it?" Tom asked, despite feeling he already knew.

"It's Father," Cristy said. "He wants to talk to you. He's waiting just outside."

"Yeah," Tom said, his voice turning vaguely hoarse. "Alright. Bring him in here."

"In private, Tom. So we'll be leaving." She threw Corben a pointed look, and he got to his feet, silently scuttling out. If Tom hadn't known his father stood in the hall just beyond, he would've called a remark after Corben about his haste.

Tom's fingers closed around his silver amulet. He muttered, "Thanks for the backup, pal."

"Tom," Cristy said with a sigh, "don't look so scared. I know he can be hard to get along with, but he's not *that* bad."

"I don't look *scared*," Tom retorted, trying his best to sound offended, but his heart wasn't in it. His attempts at bravado faded. Instead, he stared at the sheets pulled up to his waist and said, "Maybe he's not that bad for *you*, Cristy. You're not his only son."

"Well, you'll have to talk to him at some point, so you might as well get it over with. After this, you're going home to Dragon's Lair, until the royals contact Father with your punishment – which you *are* being punished. But you still heal like nothing I've ever seen, so you'll be fine in a few days. Even if you think Father isn't looking after you, clearly the gods are."

"To Dragon's Lair?" Tom echoed, barely hearing the rest. "Why not the manor in Illikon?"

"Tom, you're the Prince. You must go back to your own castle *sometimes*. We all know you love Illikon. You don't need to beat it into anyone else's head by staying here and not managing your own lands."

Tom snorted. "You say that like Father even lets me take part in the rulership instead of butting me out whenever I lift a finger. My time's better spent in Illikon where I can make a difference."

"*Anyway*," Cristy said, "I'll let him in. Good luck with him, Tom. I'm taking a break from this place so I can go home with you afterward."

Tom smiled about that, at least. He always enjoyed her company. Cristy seemed satisfied that he did, smiling back – but with that, she let in Earl Warren, who was the epitome of a regal and stern Imperial father. He wore a perfectly tailored red-and-white tunic. His equally as perfect hair and close beard, both neatly trimmed and dark but dusted with silver, completed his air of nobility. Stern, severe features and lines creased into his gracefully aging face told tales of how many scoldings he'd delivered, while several scars told how many battles he'd seen.

Warren's eyes locked with Tom's own. Even when Cristy left, Warren didn't spare her a look, as it would mean removing his glower from Tom. Whenever Warren did this to him, Tom felt like his father stared into his naked soul. It wasn't a comfortable feeling. The nearer Warren drew to the sickbed, the harder Tom avoided meeting his gaze. He looked instead at the small dragon amulet around Warren's neck, which was an exact replica of Tom's silver one but made of gold and on a golden chain.

"Thomakos," said Warren, "I'm glad you're alright."

The stone-cold, stone-hard look in Warren's dark blue eyes softened somewhat. Tom felt a twinge of guilt for occasionally thinking ill of his foster father. How was it possible that, after all these years, he still didn't know how to feel about Warren – or how to even talk to him? He didn't *want* to disrespect his father, but sometimes... He pushed the thoughts aside.

"Me too," Tom said quietly.

"I understand your frustration with Cassian besting you at the tournament, especially considering he did so in such a brutal manner..." Warren's voice hardened again. "But what were you planning before McShane restrained you?"

"I wasn't going to kill him, if that's what you're asking."

"Yes, you were. I saw the way you moved. I saw the look on your face, Thomakos. Even after all these years and so much disciplining, your temper remains uncontrollable. The other families will talk about your Nordling blood again after this, call you some kind of berserker..."

"While still blindly denying that almost everyone living in the Northwest has *some* Northrim blood in them..."

"That's beside the point." Warren leaned forward without sitting on the bed or even touching it, staring ever deeper into Tom's eyes. "You *must* restrain yourself, before you do something my entire bloodline will regret. Remember whom you represent."

"Our bloodline traces back to pureblooded dragons – I don't think they would put up with this crap. But *I* need to learn restraint because I got angry at another knight for trying to *kill* me, is that it?"

"No. Because you tried to kill *him*, and you would have succeeded, had McShane not interfered. You should thank him generously for that. Not even the royal family could save you from your fate, had you taken Cassian's life. Revenge is not the way of a knight, neither in the heat of battle nor long-plotted vengeance. If you could have seen yourself on the field today, you would realize the urgency for you to learn self-control."

Feeling a surge of anger, Tom snapped before he realized it, "I'm not the one who broke an oath to the Queen."

"Didn't you? You swore not to harm him."

"I swore not to harm him *as long as he didn't harm me.* I didn't break my oath. Besides," he added under his breath, "I didn't actually hurt the idiot anyway..."

Now it was Warren's turn to snap. "Damn it all, Thomakos, can you be serious for even one moment?"

Tom showed his hands in surrender. "I *am* being serious!"

"You acted like a mad beast out there. Everyone saw it – even the royalty!"

"I'd like to see how *you'd* react if someone broke a lance on *your* face! *On purpose!*"

"You should have known Cassian would try something. If there is one area in which you've never disappointed, it's your prowess in battle." The scowl creasing Warren's face deepened. "I have seen you lose jousts, but you always lost fairly and respected your better."

"Oh, so now Marks is my *better* for trying to kill me?"

"No, but he *did* win."

"He only won," Tom said through his teeth, "because he cheated."

"Even if that is true, you let your anger cloud your judgment, and that removed your guard. Giving in to your rage in the first place allowed this to happen. I want you to *learn* from this."

"Are you kidding me?" Tom finally released the amulet around his neck. "There's just no satisfying you, is there? I've got to be *perfect*."

"Perfect? No. But you could have shown everyone you were a better knight than Cassian by simply walking off that field. Instead, you *attacked* him."

"Yeah, I get it," answered Tom, keeping his voice controlled now. "I've heard it all before, so spare me the rest of the lecture."

Warren raised his head subtly. "I should spare you nothing. Continue down this path, and you will disgrace this family – and I will wonder if I should have left you on the streets. Am I making myself clear?"

Tom's gaze dropped. "Yes, Father."

Without another word, Warren spun on his heel to leave. But once his hand touched the doorknob, he hesitated and looked over his shoulder at Tom.

In uncharacteristic silence, Tom only stared.

"The King requested my presence when they speak with Cassian," said Warren, "so Cristina and McShane will take you back to the manor. When I return, we will depart for Dragon's Lair. Count your blessings that King Aetius and Queen Carlisa did not choose to have you spend tonight in the dungeon with Cassian. Whatever other punishment they choose will be forthcoming, I'm sure." Warren opened the door before he finished quietly, "And I'm glad you're alright, Thomakos."

The instant those words left his mouth, he was gone.

That evening, Tom found himself in his room once more. He awaited Warren's word that they would leave for Dragon's Lair, castle of House Drake. The hour was late, but Tom knew Warren would likely leave anyway. That was fine by him; he always had enjoyed the night.

Tom guessed he'd never hear the extent of Cassian's punishments, nor would he hear what was in store for him until his wound healed enough to, most likely, perform extensive menial servant labor around Castle Illikon. If he was lucky, he'd avoid a turn in the dungeons, but he wouldn't protest if that order came. Other nobles would surely shout about favoritism, but Tom didn't care.

Whatever punishment Cassian received, Tom knew the scar his actions had left on the Marks family name would fade with time... unlike the scar that stared at Tom in his reflection: a long, deep mark on his left forehead, slicing into his hairline. Another reminder of assorted failures.

But it didn't hurt as badly as his father's words. His relationship with Warren had always been unstable, but it only ever seemed to get worse.

Rain drummed again on the windows of Tom's room. The beautiful red and gold carpet and bed, the intricate frescos, the magnificent armor on its stand... Tonight, it felt cold and unwelcoming. Tom gazed, alone, out the window past the sheets of rain. Through the glass, his view distorted by rainwater, Tom made out the moon's baleful visage hanging over the sea, ominously looking out amidst gathering storm-clouds.

Tom removed his amulet, staring at the dragon in his palm. Lightning flashed. The silver shimmered briefly in its purple-white glow. His family's heraldic dragon, same as the ones on his armor, looked ever proud and fearsome.

Tom opened the drawer of his nightstand and placed the amulet inside, shoving it closed again. Tonight marked the first time he had taken it off, save for bathing. The moment he shut the drawer, he felt as though a part of him was missing – but he didn't open it again.

His eyes were drawn to the nearly-full moon. It brought back memories of another night with a moon just as bright... the night he'd earned his Demon Slayer title. Perhaps what bothered him most of the rumors Cassian spread was that many were based in truth.

The King and Queen had personally sent him after the magi Cassian had mentioned, for one of the mages had been their own blood. They had trusted Tom, whose loyalty was to Illikon before the Empire itself, to spare the boy and keep their secret, saving him from the Imperial Inquisition – an order that would either have imprisoned or executed the boy for his magic. Carrying out the mission had cost Tom much pain and even death... for it had cost him his own squire, Radek.

But in the end, he'd slain the demon, on a night much like this one – and he had let an entire cult of mages go free. Because, when he'd found them, he pitied them. Magic was illegal in the Empire, but they had never asked for their magic. They'd simply been born with it.

One of the mage girls had given him a ring, the same one Cassian had jeered at before. Tom looked down at the band of twisted gold.

That night that felt like so long ago now.

He would never forget her smile when she'd given him the ring, so happy to be free. Tom tried not to think about freedom as he opened the drawer long enough to deposit the ring with his amulet. Bickering noble houses, surrounded by pomp and pretense, always struggling for favor and prestige, felt like a petty game that he was stuck playing against his will – yet it was worth it to be a knight. Knowing that the sight of him brought hope to the people of the Northwest...

Heroism returned his thoughts to the demon of Wrath. Mortals were never meant to fight demons at all, much less alone. But he had done it, and he'd won. Ash and smoke had turned the very air into a choking hellscape, impossibly hot, like some slice of another world. He felt it again, the heat on his skin, burning his eyes... and burning something deeper inside him. Merely being in the demon's presence would have been enough to drive most people mad with terror.

"Let me feel your rage, *mortal,"* the demon had said, its voice unearthly, so hideous and unnatural his ears all but blocked it out – and so the words had twisted into his very soul instead. *"Without it, you will never defeat me. Without it, you are nothing."*

Tom twitched and forced the demon's voice from his mind again. It had told him to give in, and he had. That was how he'd become the Demon Slayer, a title almost no currently living mortal man could boast.

He watched a storm gather on the horizon, adding more instability to the already ominous black waves of the sea. Thunder growled in the distance. Wind howled over the manor. The wild sounds of nature chased away thoughts of failure, noble houses, and demons. A part of him wished he was out there in the storm, fighting for his life, doing battle with an enemy far more honest than politics.

The door to his room creaked open. In peered an elderly house servant, who said, "Prince Tom? Your father has summoned you. He says it's time to go."

Tom finally pried his eyes from the moon. "Thank you," he replied, running his fingers over his neck that felt barren without his family amulet, yet he still didn't retrieve it. "I'm ready."

The sun was up. Lieutenant Corben McShane shouldn't even have been working, yet he stood over a corpse.

He touched the dead man gingerly with the toe of his boot. Corben hadn't known the dead watchman personally, but he'd seen him around. Now he barely recognized him, crumpled lifeless on a street in Illikon's slums, drying in the sun.

Corben addressed another watchman, "You found him like this – armor stripped?"

The other watchman in question was a comrade and drinking buddy of Corben's named Wattie. He pointed to the cellar door beside them and replied, "And stuffed up in there. The building's abandoned. I was checking it for a runaway thief when I stumbled across this instead."

The third man at the scene, an old watchman with a grey-brown beard and watery eyes, shook his head sadly. "I liked Pate. Here I figured he stowed away on some ship to get out of his gambling debts, but the poor sod gave his life in the line of duty."

Corben nodded. "Almost makes you wanna think better o' people."

The older man took a long draw from a bottle he carried. Any other watchmen would've been reprimanded for drinking on the job, but not Baldric, for he was the *'Praefectus Vigilum,'* Captain of the Watch.

Corben leaned over, inspecting the body. Old blood coated the dead man's neck, chin, and much of his front. He'd bled freely from ugly, ragged wounds ripped across his throat. His limbs were twisted – he'd been stuffed away while still freshly dead, and only after had his body gone stiff.

"Killed a couple days ago – his throat's torn open," Corben noted aloud. "No other wounds, and I'll be damned if his face doesn't still look startled. A real pro job, quick and clean, 'cept this doesn't look like a blade did it. But if it wasn't a knife, I don't know what it was."

Such wounds made him think of claws. Corben dared not offer such an insane theory out loud. He'd only seen claw wounds once in his life, having always lived in the city, and they'd been under unique circumstances, during the appearance of that demon...

"Any ideas?" Captain Baldric asked.

"No one from this town. I know the scum in my town, and none of 'em are half this good. Not that's still around, anyway."

"Someone from the docks, come in on a ship?" ventured Wattie.

Corben ran a hand over his shaved head, spotting something nearby. "Maybe, but I keep a close eye on that lot... Hang on a minute."

They were in a secluded area of Illikon's slums, down a narrow old street that hardly saw use. Grasses of the Illikon Plains threatened to reclaim the stones underfoot, bursting up between the cracks. Corben walked across the road to an alley opposite the building where they found Pate's corpse – and sprinted into the shadows after a shape there.

Corben snatched the figure by the collar. Turned out his catch was a homeless old peasant. Corben's fellow watchmen jogged over as Corben dumped the hairy beggar onto the street in plain view.

"Why're you trying to run, old man?" said Corben.

The beggar pulled at his thin, greying beard. "I dunno – reflex, I guess! I didn't do nothin' or see nothin', I swear by all the gods!"

"I saw enough fish bones back there for several days' worth o' meals. You've been here a while, maybe even when that watchman was killed."

The man made a pitiful attempt to shield his head with his skinny arms. "I didn't kill nobody, sir, not in my whole life, I swear!"

"I know you didn't kill Pate, old codger. I don't think you could move fast enough. But maybe you saw who did."

Corben tightened his leather brawling gloves, but Captain Baldric stepped forward and put a hand on Corben's thick arm. Corben let his hands drop, watching Baldric kneel and pass his bottle to the old beggar. The old man didn't hesitate to take a sip. Once he had, he cleared his throat and licked his lips, like the ale restored his power of speech.

"Thanks," he said. "I did see something, but you boys wouldn't believe me. You'd say I was drunk, or addled, or..."

The captain nodded patiently. "Whatever you saw, it's more than what we have right now. Tell us."

"Aye, sir, but you won't like it. I saw a man, a big man, hell he was so tall I'd think he was north o' the Nordlings – and this... girl, she seemed small, short. Just a slight little thing. She struck me as– as odd, almost... *fey*. Funny pair they were, one so big and one so small. Like something out of a storybook. Thought I was seein' things. Then along comes the guard, and... and I dunno what happened exactly, sir, but they all got into a kind of scuffle. Then the big man, all I could see was black, just black, like he was a livin' shadow—"

Corben rolled his eyes, waiting for the drama to pass and the facts to come out. So far, the old man was right about one thing: Corben figured he was completely addled.

"And... and they fought, not long mind you, it all happened so fast, and then... well..."

His voice drifted – and changed.

"That's when it happened. The... th-the demon."

Though Corben had chuckled at the fairy-tale about the shade and the fey girl, the word 'demon' gave him a chill. He crouched and rested a hand on the beggar's bony shoulder, which felt frail under his touch. Corben looked the man right in the eyes.

"Now hang on, old timer," he said. "You better not be pullin' our leg with this demon business. I've *seen* a demon. Barely lived to tell it. So *don't joke* about demons. I'll know, and I won't laugh."

The apple in the old man's throat bobbed. "I wouldn't dream of it, sir! I saw one too, Zeus be my witness! It... it... the man, the shade, he turned into a demon before my very eyes! He... he got mad, and out came these wings, great clawed wings, and it had a tail with a spade like all the stories say – and it killed the watchman quicker than anything! And then it... *he*... he looked right at me— gods, his eyes... Full o' dark magic they were, this purple like darkness given color. Like evil itself. I felt naked – not o' clothes, but o' skin and flesh and bone – just a naked soul looking at the hellfire wink off the grim reaper's scythe."

Baldric grunted. "Poetic. Maybe he's a writer, and that's why he's out here starving and alone. Does this sound like your demon, McShane?"

Corben just watched the old beggar, who'd gone pale as a sheet. He no longer looked at any of them. He gazed into thin air with his eyes focused on nothing. He'd since curled up like a frightened child, rocking himself.

"Not exactly," Corben said at length, "and that demon is long gone, so it's not that one, either. But... the eyes. What he said about the eyes is dead on. Pray to the gods you never look a demon in the eye, Cap'n. What he just said – I've seen it. Sometimes I still do. And yet... I don't know. I almost wanna believe him, but I just can't. No way another demon's ended up in Illikon. That's the stuff o' legends – and nightmares."

Wattie gave a nervous laugh. "Well, either way, thank the gods you're here, McShane. At least the Watch has someone who knows how to fight them."

"No it doesn't, Wat. All I did was watch from a boat far away. There's only one man in Illikon who knows how to fight a demon, and he's got more on his mind than a dead watchman and an old man seein' things. If this *does* turn out to be a demon," Corben crossed his arms, "*then* I'll bother him with it... but that demon he slew did somethin' to Tom's mind. He ain't been the same since."

Baldric blinked. "So – you're not going to tell him?"

Corben gave him a long look. "No. Until we can prove it, this is our problem, not Tom's or any other knight's... and I get the feeling Tom's got enough to worry about."

Author Note

Thank you for reading one of my books! I hope you enjoyed it. If you stick with Wulfgard, and especially with my work, you'll be seeing a lot more of Kye as well as his target, Tom Drake, among other characters.

I also hope you will pick up the book into which this story ties: *Wulfgard: Knightfall*, the first in *The Prophecy of the Six* series. Of my work, it is dearest to my heart. I promise it will be worth it to read the series in its entirety.

I have always wanted to tell my stories, and while it has its many hardships, I've finally settled into self-publishing books such as this one. My brother, Justin R. R. Stebbins – who also illustrated this book – and I have worked virtually our whole lives on this universe, and my characters and their stories mean everything to me. I'm very happy you found your way here to some of my many tales told in the world of Wulfgard.

While storytelling is my deepest passion, I have an endless fascination with many subjects, including filmmaking, history, folklore, mythology, and much more. All of these affect my writing methods as well as the stories I tell and the worlds in which my characters exist. I dream of working in a more visual medium, especially to tell the tale of *The Prophecy of the Six*: the story that means the most to me.

For many years, my brother and I have worked to ensure a certain level of historical accuracy and attention to detail in the world of Wulfgard, paying close attention to our incorporation of real-world myth and legend alongside our original concepts. Although Wulfgard is not set in the real world, it is inspired by a different take on history and mythology, combined with original aspects.

Once again, I hope you enjoyed the book and that you will explore my other and future works. If you like my work, please help spread the word to others who may be interested and leave this book, and my other books you might purchase, reviews across the Internet. Every new reader means a lot to me, and in the world of self-publishing, they can be very hard to find! Thank you again for another step toward making my dream come true: sharing my stories and characters with the world.

And, remember, this is only the beginning of the tale.

The stories of these characters will also continue, and many characters in this novel are also featured in other works.

Keep an eye out for many more novels, novellas, short story collections, and graphic novels, and be sure to read the *The Prophecy of the Six* series, beginning with *Knightfall*.

Continue exploring the world of Wulfgard

For more Wulfgard books, comics, and stories, be sure to visit me and my brother online at:

WWW.WULFGARD.NET

And visit me online at:

MAVERICK-WEREWOLF.COM

Scan this QR code to sign up for my newsletter! Be the first to hear about new releases, upcoming books, and much more. Details at the link.

<u>Wulfgard:</u> Knightfall

A Novel by Maegan A. Stebbins

Illustrated by Justin R. R. Stebbins

Rage.

Few can match the fury of Sir Tom Drake in battle - not even a Demon of Wrath. When Tom killed just such a fiend in single combat, a feat of which most mortals would never dream, he became the Demon Slayer. To the people of his beloved city of Illikon, Tom is a hero. But his city swears fealty to the Achaean Empire, and to them, he is just another knight.

Enter Sir Scaevius, Left Hand of the Emperor. With war raging against a barbarian alliance massing to the North, Scaevius takes command of Illikon's armies and orders Tom on a suicide mission. Tom obeys, but not without protest.

Soon, he finds himself fighting not only the barbarians, but his own superiors as well – and something else, something supernatural.

A monster is stalking him: a half man, half beast abomination from legend... a werewolf. It haunts his dreams and even his waking hours, and he starts to suffer blackouts, unsure what is real and what is nightmare. Hated by his superiors, hunted by beasts and assassins, Tom Drake must fight for his home, his life, and even his mind. The events that are about to unfold will change his life, and the world, forever.

A thrilling tale of adventure, dashing heroics, chilling horror, alluring mystery, and both personal duels and epic battles centered around memorable characters, *Knightfall* takes you to the edge of your seat in a wild ride set in a traditional dark age heroic fantasy world, where all myths are true – and monsters from legend seek to devour Men. Meet the sharply characterized cast, discover a new realm at once dark yet not without light and hope, and return to fantasy's roots in the series *The Prophecy of the Six* and the world of Wulfgard.

Wulfgard:
Into the North
A Graphic Novel by Justin R. R. Stebbins

In Northrim, a Wanderer stumbles down from the Jagged Edge after a long journey, and runs into a werewolf. In the Imperial capital, a young elven thief finds herself caught by demons and assassins hunting for a set of mysterious ancient artifacts. In the city of Rimegard, a princess struggles to hide a terrifying secret. And in the darkness beneath the world, a clan of dwarves wage war with demonic dark elves. Soon, all their fates are destined to intertwine. This volume of comics introduces their stories, comprising the first four chapters of a much larger tale.

Special Thanks

...to my mother, Mary, and for her assistance in reading over my work; my father, Jack; and my amazing brothers, Justin and Ryan; always. Without you, the world of Wulfgard would not have been created.

And many more special thanks to all my patrons, including but not limited to...
Ajestice
Alex
Caleb Blanchet
Jared Buniel
Heckogecko
Jan Lingenfelder
Valerie Lingenfelder
Darren Persad
Kyle "Ambad" Smith

And still more special thanks to the following professors for their kindness, encouragement, faith in me, and honest and critical assessments of my work. Thank you for sharing your many fields of expertise with me for the historically inspired concepts and cultures featured in this book and Wulfgard at large.

Dr. Frederic J. Baumgartner
Dr. Peter W. Graham
Dr. Shoshana Milgram Knapp
Dr. Karen Swenson

Other Works

This book list was current at the time of this book's publication and may not accurately reflect my current published works. Visit my website for an up-to-date list.

Set in the world of Wulfgard

The following books take place along a particular timeline, as they exist in the same world.

Knightfall begins my main series in the setting and remains the best starting point.

This list is in chronological order, though some take place in roughly the same time. Most do not directly tie together. There is no "required reading" unless a work is noted as a sequel.

- *Djedar Rath, Book I: The Tomb of Ankhu*
- *Djedar Rath, Book II: The Curse of Ankhu* (coming 2025)
- *The Hunt Never Ends*
- *Tales of Wulfgard, Volume I*
- *The Demon's Fang*
- *The Prophecy of the Six, Book I: Knightfall*

Nonfiction/Academic/Research works

- *The Werewolf: Past and Future – Lycanthropy's Lost History and Modern Devolution*
- *The Book of Were-Wolves* by Sabine Baring-Gould, edited, annotated, and translated by Maegan A. Stebbins
- *Werewolf Folklore Stories: Real-World Tales of Lycanthropy Throughout History* (coming 2025-26)
- *Werewolf Facts* (coming soon)

www.ingramcontent.com/pod-product-compliance
Lightning Source LLC
Chambersburg PA
CBHW022022170626
46808CB00003B/1019